Jamison pulled **S0-ARO-945**
U.S. Army pen from his coat pocket and kept his face impassive as he thought of questions that begged to be answered.

Why'd you leave me, Michele? What happened that made you run away?

Shoving them aside, he asked, "Did you see anything out of place, Miss Logan, before you noticed the body?"

"Miss Logan?" She narrowed her gaze. Evidently she didn't understand his decision to forgo first names.

No matter how alluring Michele might be, Jamison needed to remain professional but aloof and firmly grounded in the present.

"The room was dark...the smell of blood. I—I saw Yolanda," she said.

"What happened next?"

"Someone shoved me into the couch."

Jamison tensed. His mouth went dry. He swallowed, knowing all too well what the killer could have done to Michele. "Can...can you describe the person?"

She shook her head. "He struck me from behind. I never saw him, *Agent Steele.*"

Jamison almost smiled at her attempt to play hardball. Evidently she didn't realize he'd built a wall around his heart and added armor for protection.

Books by Debby Giusti

Love Inspired Suspense

DEBBY GIUSTI

is a medical technologist who loves working with test tubes and petri dishes almost as much as she loves to write. Growing up as an army brat, Debby met and married her husband—then a captain in the army—at Fort Knox, Kentucky. Together they traveled the world, raised three wonderful army brats of their own and have now settled in Atlanta, Georgia, where Debby spins tales of suspense that touch the heart and soul. Contact Debby through her website, www.DebbyGiusti.com, email debby@debbygiusti.com, or write c/o Love Inspired Suspense, 233 Broadway, Suite 1001, New York, NY 10279.

The Colonel's Daughter

Debby Giusti

Love Inspired

Recycling programs
for this product may
not exist in your area.

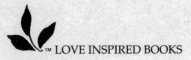

™ LOVE INSPIRED BOOKS

ISBN-13: 978-0-373-44501-1

THE COLONEL'S DAUGHTER

www.LoveInspiredBooks.com

Printed in U.S.A.

Therefore everyone who hears these words of mine
and puts them into practice is like a wise man
who built his house on the rock. The rain
came down, the streams rose, and the winds blew
and beat against that house; yet it did not fall,
because it had its foundation on the rock.
—*Matthew 7:24, 25*

This book is dedicated to
the deployed members of our Armed Forces
and to the families who await their return.
To my husband, who has always been my hero.
To Liz, Joe, Mary, Eric, Katie, Anna, Robert,
William and John Anthony.
To the parishioners at Holy Trinity
who encourage me to write more stories.
To the Seekers and the extended Seekerville family
for your friendship and support.
To Anna Adams with gratitude
for our weekly meetings at Panera's.
To Emily Rodmell, my editor,
and Deidre Knight, my agent.

ONE

Angry storm clouds turned the evening sky over Fort Rickman, Georgia, as dark as the mood within the car. Michele Logan pulled her eyes from the road and glanced at her mother, sitting next to her in the passenger seat.

Roberta Logan, usually the poised colonel's wife, toyed with the collar of her blouse and gave voice to a subject that had weighed on Michele's heart for the past two years. "Despite what you think, dear, you haven't gotten over your brother's death."

Ever since she and her mother had left her parents' quarters en route to the potluck dinner, Roberta had insisted on talking about the accident that had claimed Lance's life. The topic added to Michele's anxiety, especially with the inclement August weather and the darkening night.

"Aren't you the one who insists life goes on, Mother?"

"And it does, dear, but that doesn't mean you've worked through your grief." Roberta turned her gaze toward the encroaching storm. "As I've told you before, you weren't to blame."

True enough that Michele wasn't to blame for the crashed army helicopter, yet she still felt responsible for her brother's death. If she had visited that weekend, he never would have been on board the fateful flight.

"I don't like the looks of those clouds." Distracted by the storm, Roberta worried her fingers. "Maybe Yolanda should have canceled the potluck."

"And disappoint the wives in Dad's brigade? You said it's important for the women to come together socially when the men were deployed."

"But the weatherman mentioned another line of storms moving into Georgia." Her mother's voice grew increasingly concerned. "You should have stayed in Atlanta until the bad weather passed, dear."

"I told you I want to help with preparations for the brigade's return to Fort Rickman."

"Which won't be for another week. The real reason you came home early is to visit the cemetery tomorrow. It's been two years. You don't need to spend each anniversary crying at Lance's grave site."

"I'm not crying."

"But you will be tomorrow." Roberta shifted in the seat and sighed. "You never should have left post in the first place."

Although she wouldn't admit it, Michele sometimes wondered if moving to Atlanta ten months ago had been a mistake. She hadn't seen Jamison Steele in all that time, but she'd thought about him far too often. They had dated for almost a year, and she had believed he was everything she'd wanted in a guy. When an investigation turned deadly on post, she realized her mistake.

As if sensing her struggle, Roberta gazed knowingly at her daughter. "Your father and I would love to have you move back, dear. You could work from home."

"I…I can't."

Roberta rubbed her hand over Michele's shoulder. "Just think about it."

Moving back wasn't an option. Michele had made a

new life for herself. One that didn't involve the military. She was happy in Atlanta, or so she kept telling herself.

Droplets of rain spattered against the windshield as Michele turned into the Buckner Housing Area. She activated the wipers and flipped the lights to high beam, exposing broken twigs and leaves that had fallen in the last downpour.

The street was long and narrow and led to a two-story home at the dead end of a cul-de-sac surrounded by a thick forest of hardwoods and tall pines. Michele pulled to the curb in front of the dark quarters.

Mrs. Logan eyed the house completely devoid of light. "Yolanda must have lost power in the storm." Thunder rumbled overhead, and fat raindrops pummeled the car.

"I'll get the casserole, Mother. You make a run for the door." Michele grabbed the ceramic dish from the backseat and raced behind her mother to the covered porch.

Roberta tapped twice with the brass knocker. When no one answered, she glanced questioningly at Michele and then pushed the door open.

"Yolanda, it's Roberta and Michele. We're early, but we wanted to help before the others arrive." Roberta stepped inside and motioned Michele to follow. A bolt of lightning sizzled across the sky. A second later, thunder shook the house.

An earthy smell wafted past Michele. She closed the door and looked left into the dining area. Flames from two large candles flickered over the linen tablecloth, highlighting the plates and silverware stacked on the sideboard.

"Yolanda, where are you?" Roberta walked toward the kitchen, her heels clipping over the hardwood floor.

Michele placed the casserole on the dining table before she returned to the foyer. At the opposite end of the hallway, her mother stopped short, hands on her hips.

"Yolanda?"

Roberta's raised voice and insistent call twisted more than a ripple of concern along Michele's spine. A sense of foreboding flooded over her as intense as any she had felt for her father in the twelve months of his deployment. With the silent quarters closing in around her, she was now equally worried about Yolanda.

A floorboard creaked in the living room. Michele turned toward the sound. The settling house, the wind howling down the chimney...or was someone there?

She crossed the hallway, drawn by a need to discover not only the source of the noise but also the mineral smell that increased in intensity the closer she got to the living room. Her neck tingled, but she ignored the warning and stepped toward the oversized couch and love seat that filled the center of the living area.

A small table and chair sat nestled in an alcove behind the love seat. Michele tried to make out the dark outline on the pale carpet.

"Yolanda?" From the kitchen, Roberta called one more time. Her voice was filled with question and a tremble that signified she, too, sensed something was wrong.

Michele's pulse quickened as her eyes adjusted to the darkness. Newspapers lay scattered around an overturned lamp.

Her stomach tightened.

A roar filled her ears. She stepped around the couch and saw the woman lying in a pool of blood.

"No!" Michele's hand flew to her throat in the exact spot where Yolanda's neck had been cut.

A rustle sounded behind her. Before she could turn, a violent force lunged into her. She crashed against the back of the couch. Her ribs took the blow. Pain exploded along her side and mixed with air that whooshed from her lungs. She gasped, and for an instant saw only darkness.

Retreating footsteps sounded in the hallway.

Her mother screamed.

Michele fisted her hands and willed herself to remain conscious. A door slammed shut in the rear of the house.

Still gasping for air, she struggled to her feet and stumbled out of the living area, her only thought to find her mother and make sure she was alive.

Lightning turned the darkness bright for one terrifying second. Roberta lay slumped against the wall.

Dropping to her knees, Michele touched her mother's shoulder. "Mama?"

Roberta moaned. Her eyes blinked open.

Relief rushed over Michele along with a wave of nausea. She hung her head to stave off the passing sickness and dug in her pocket for her cell phone.

A face flashed through her mind. Without weighing the consequences, she punched Speed Dial for a number she should have deleted ten months ago.

He answered on the second ring.

"Criminal Investigation Division, Fort Rickman, Georgia. This is Special Agent Jamison Steele."

The memory of his warm embrace and tender kisses washed over her. For one sweet, illogical second, she felt safe.

"Hello?" He waited for a response.

"Jamison—"

A sharp intake of air. "Michele?"

"I need help." Rubbing her free hand over her forehead, she tried to focus. "I'm at Quarters 122. In the Buckner Housing Area. Contact the military police."

"What happened?"

"One of the wives… Her husband's in Afghanistan.

He's in my father's brigade. She was hosting a potluck for the brigade wives. Someone broke in—"

Jamison issued a series of commands to a person in his office. "I'm on the way, Michele. The military police are being notified. I'll be there in three minutes. Are you hurt?"

"I…I'm okay. It's Yolanda Hughes."

Michele swallowed down the lump that filled her throat. "Yolanda's dead."

Heart in his throat, Jamison pulled to the curb and hit the ground running, weapon in one hand, Maglite in the other.

Stay calm. Ignoring the internal advice, his gut tightened when he stepped into the house and spied Michele on the floor with her arm around her mother.

For an instant, he was once again the man who loved Michele more than anything. Swallowing hard, Jamison shoved aside any lingering hope for a future together, a future that had died when she walked out of his life.

Raw fear flashed from her blue eyes and cut through his resolve to remain neutral. Ten months ago, her smile had lit up his world. Today Michele's face was as pale as death and furrowed with pain.

Head buried in her daughter's shoulder, Mrs. Logan cried softly. Michele nudged her gently. "Jamison's here, Mama."

The older woman glanced up, her eyes red and swollen. "Oh, Jamison. Yolanda… A man raced past me and out the back door. I…I tried to stop him."

"Did he hurt you?" His gaze fell on Michele. Tousled brown hair hung around her oval face.

"We're both a little bruised. Nothing serious. But

Yolanda—" Unable to continue, Michele raised a trembling hand and pointed to the living area.

"Stay where you are," he cautioned, struggling to remain objective. "The ambulance is on its way."

A rank, coppery smell greeted Jamison as he entered the living room. He aimed his light over the blood that had soaked into the thick carpet, blackening the fibers.

His gut twisted at the tragic sight.

The victim was an African-American female. Probably mid- to late-thirties. Shoulder-length brown hair. Dark eyes wide open. The look of terror etched on her face.

A deep laceration had severed her carotid artery. Massive blood loss pooled under her upper torso.

Kneeling beside the woman, he felt for a pulse, yet knew full well life had been heinously snatched from Yolanda Hughes. Her wrist was supple and still warm. No rigor mortis. Not yet.

He tried the light switch, then played the Maglite over the living room. His gaze settled ever so briefly on the family photograph above the mantel. The deceased was smiling warmly, her hands on the shoulders of a man in uniform. Major's rank on his epaulets. Two children. A boy and girl.

The dread of finding the children dead roared through Jamison. He strode back to the hallway. "Mrs. Hughes had kids?"

Michele held up her hand, palm out. "They're at the Graysons'. Lieutenant Colonel Grayson is my father's executive officer. The two families are close. The Grayson kids invited Benjamin and Natalie to stay with them tonight."

Breathing out a sigh of relief, Jamison moved quickly into the kitchen and edged open the back door. He stepped outside and studied the darkness, knowing the killer was long gone.

Retracing his steps, Jamison headed toward the flickering candlelight and checked the dining area before he scurried up the stairs to the second floor. Sirens screamed in the distance.

Finding nothing out of place and no one upstairs, he returned to the main landing and ensured that Michele and her mother were all right before he opened the front door and stepped onto the porch. Three military police cars screeched to the curb. An ambulance followed close behind. Across the street, neighbors came out of their homes and stared with worried expressions at the activity.

Jamison directed the military police. "The victim's in the living room, first floor. Two children are spending the night with friends. Husband is deployed. Colonel Logan's wife and daughter are in the hallway and need medical attention. The electricity is down. Get some temporary lighting in there ASAP."

A military policeman began to cordon off the area with crime scene tape.

"Someone go door to door," Jamison ordered. "Question the neighbors. See if anyone saw anything suspicious."

"Roger that, sir." A stocky military policeman motioned for another MP to join him, and the twosome hustled to a nearby set of quarters.

The medics raced up the front steps. Jamison followed them inside. One man moved into the living area. The other two knelt beside Mrs. Logan and Michele.

Assured they were being adequately cared for, Jamison returned to the porch to oversee the bevy of activity. A young military policeman approached him.

"Sir, the power line to the house appears to have been severed. The on-post maintenance company has been notified. They're sending someone to fix the line."

"Dust for prints first."

"Roger that, sir."

"How long until he arrives?"

"They said he'd be here shortly."

"Did they give you an exact time?"

"No, sir."

A car pulled into the driveway. CID special agent Dawson Timmons—a tall blond with a thick neck—climbed onto the sidewalk. Favoring his right leg, he approached Jamison, who quickly filled him in.

"What do you need me to do?" Dawson asked.

"Take care of the crime scene. I want to question Mrs. Logan and her daughter and get them out of here as soon as possible. The victim was hosting a potluck for the brigade wives. The guests should be arriving soon. Talk to them individually to see if they have information pertinent to the case."

"How many ladies are we expecting?"

"Eighteen plates were stacked on a table in the dining room."

Dawson glanced at the unit insignia plaque on the front door. "First Brigade, Fifth Infantry Division should be home next week."

Jamison nodded. "Contact Lieutenant Colonel Grayson, the unit's executive officer, in Afghanistan. Tell him I need to talk to Colonel Logan. Once the other wives arrive, word about the murder will get out. I don't want Major Hughes to learn what happened to his wife via Twitter or Facebook."

As Dawson placed the call, Jamison reentered the house. Huge battery-operated floodlights illuminated the earlier darkened interior. The medics had moved Mrs. Logan and Michele to the kitchen, where the women sat at the small breakfast table.

Mrs. Logan sported a bandage on her forehead and stared up at one of the EMTs. "If my blood pressure is okay after all that, young man, I'm not going to the hospital. But I appreciate your advice and the excellent care you've provided tonight."

"I still think you and Miss Logan should have a doctor check you, ma'am."

Michele stood and stepped toward Jamison, her voice low when she spoke. "Mother insists she's okay, although I'd feel better if a doctor looked her over."

"Are you planning to take your own advice?" Frustrated by Michele's attempt to slip back into their old familiarity, Jamison realized his tone was sharp.

She stared at him for a long moment, then turned and walked back to her seat. "If Mother has any problems, we'll reconsider her decision."

She was closing herself off from him. Again. He shouldn't be surprised. Being with Michele drove home the point Jamison had known for months. The colonel's daughter wasn't for him. She had left him high and dry without as much as a so long, see you later. He thought he had healed, but tonight the memory festered like an open wound.

"Jamison, any clue who the murderer might be?" Mrs. Logan asked once the medics had cleared the room. Her face was blotched, but she seemed more in control than she had been earlier.

"No, ma'am. But I ordered a post lockdown on the way over here. No one goes on or off Fort Rickman until the military police search the garrison. Right now they're crisscrossing the post in an attempt to find the perpetrator."

"Curtis Hughes needs to be told."

"We're placing a call to your husband so he can personally notify Major Hughes."

Mrs. Logan nodded her approval. "I want to talk to Stanley after you do."

"Yes, ma'am."

Michele's cheeks had more color than when he'd first spotted her in the hallway, but her jaw was tight and her eyes guarded.

He pulled a small notebook and a U.S. government pen from his coat pocket and kept his face impassive as he thought of questions that begged to be answered. *Why'd you leave me, Michele? What happened that made you run away?*

Shoving them aside, he asked instead, "Did you see anything out of place, Miss Logan, before you noticed the body?"

"Miss Logan?" She narrowed her gaze and squared her shoulders in an attempt to cover the flash of confusion that clouded her face. Evidently, she didn't understand his decision to forgo first names.

No matter how alluring Michele might be, Jamison refused to expose his own inner conflict. He needed to remain professional and aloof, firmly grounded in the present.

Michele tugged at a wayward strand of hair and glanced down as if struggling to find the right words to express what had happened.

"I…I heard a noise and decided to investigate." She pulled in a deep breath. "A lamp…the room was dark… the smell of blood. Wh…when I stepped closer, I…I saw Yolanda."

"What happened next?"

"Someone shoved me into the couch."

Jamison tensed. His mouth went dry. He swallowed, knowing all too well what the killer could have done to Michele. "Can you describe the person?"

She shook her head. "He struck from behind. I never saw him."

Jamison turned to Mrs. Logan. "Did you see him, ma'am?"

"I'm afraid not. My eyes hadn't adjusted to the darkness, and everything happened so fast."

"Before entering the quarters, did either of you notice anyone outside? Or anything that seemed out of the ordinary?"

"Mother and I were talking as we drove up. I'm afraid we weren't being observant, *Agent* Steele."

Jamison almost smiled at her attempt to play hardball. Evidently, she didn't realize he'd built a wall around his heart and added armor for protection. Michele wouldn't hurt him again. He'd learned his lesson and had the scars to prove it.

"You're still working for that insurance company?" he asked.

"That's right. Patriotic Life."

"Doing risk management?"

"And working from home, if that's your next question." She crossed her legs and braced her spine, confrontation evident as she shifted positions.

The pulse in his neck throbbed. "Do you have a list of tonight's guests?"

"Mother does on her computer. I can print a copy for you."

"How many people, other than the eighteen women who were invited, may have known about the potluck?"

Michele glanced at her mother for help. "I'm not sure."

"Seventeen women and one man," Mrs. Logan corrected Jamison. "Major Shirley Yates is in charge of logistics for the brigade. Her husband, Greg, usually attends the events when we get together."

"Has he been to Mrs. Hughes's home previously?" Jamison asked.

Mrs. Logan nodded. "Yes, of course. Yolanda entertains often."

"Mr. Yates lives on post?"

"In Freemont. Greg has a son from a previous marriage, but I believe he's in college. No telling who else knew about the potluck. Yolanda probably shared the information with some of her neighbors. She scrapbooks with a group of women in her housing area. Those wives might have known."

"Had she mentioned anyone acting strangely in the neighborhood? Or had she reconnected with anyone from her past recently?"

"Not that I'm aware of."

"Is she on Facebook or Twitter?"

"Yolanda emailed her husband and kept up with the brigade news on our wives' loop. She never mentioned being on any social media sites."

"How about her marriage?" Jamison glanced at both women. "Were there problems?"

Michele forced a sad smile. "They seemed to be the perfect couple. Devoted to each other and to their children."

"Any other men in her life? An old friend?"

Mrs. Logan held up her hand. "You can stop that line of questioning, Jamison. Yolanda was a devoted wife. She adored her husband. I'll vouch for their love and their marriage."

"What about Greg Yates, the major's husband? Were he and Mrs. Hughes friendly?"

"Friends but that's all."

"And his marriage?"

Mrs. Logan dropped her gaze and thought for a moment before she spoke. "Deployments are tough, Jamison. There's been some talk, but only that."

"Meaning?"

"Meaning Shirley and Greg plan to separate once she returns home with the unit."

"How's Mr. Yates handling the situation?"

"In my opinion, he's in denial."

"And Major Yates?"

"Stanley's said she seems withdrawn."

Jamison made note of the information. "Major Yates asked for the separation?"

"Evidently Shirley told Greg she was leaving him. He suggested they go through a period of separation first." Mrs. Logan pursed her lips momentarily. "A few wives thought Shirley was interested in someone else."

"Someone in the brigade?"

"I don't know."

"Could she be involved with Major Hughes?"

Mrs. Logan's eyes widened in protest. "Absolutely not."

"Is there anything about Major Hughes that seems questionable, ma'am? As far as you know, does he get along with the other officers in the brigade? Is there anyone who might hold a grudge against him?"

"My husband has always given Curtis high praise. He went to Iraq with Stanley, when my husband commanded his battalion some years ago. Stanley was thrilled when Curtis was assigned to the First of the Fifth shortly before the brigade deployed to Afghanistan."

Jamison turned to Michele. "You've known Major and Mrs. Hughes since he worked for your father in the battalion?"

She nodded. "I used to babysit their kids. But if you think either Yolanda or her husband were involved in something that led to her death, you're wrong."

"I don't suspect anything at this point." Although he wanted to question Greg Yates. A spurned husband might retaliate against the man he perceived had stolen his wife.

Even though Mrs. Logan vouched for Major Hughes's fidelity, things happened, especially during a deployment.

Jamison closed his notebook and tucked it into his sports coat pocket. "What about the children, ma'am? Does Major Hughes have family in the area?"

"No one close by. Yolanda and Curtis are both from Missouri. I'm sure Benjamin and Natalie can stay at Erica Grayson's house until relatives arrive."

Dawson entered the kitchen. He handed the phone to Jamison. "Lieutenant Colonel Grayson is on the line."

Jamison quickly explained the reason he had phoned. Grayson relayed the information to the commander. Colonel Logan knew Jamison from when he and Michele had dated, but there would be nothing personal about tonight's call.

The commander's voice was husky with emotion when he came on the line. "Was Roberta hurt? What about Michele?"

"They're okay, sir." As much as he hated giving Colonel Logan bad news, Jamison had to be forthright. Being deployed half a world away meant the colonel couldn't protect his wife and daughter. Jamison could relate. Once upon a time, he had wanted to be the man keeping Michele safe.

"The perpetrator was in the house when Mrs. Logan and Michele arrived on the scene. Both women were shoved to the floor, sir. The medics checked them out. At this point, I don't believe they're going to need further medical care."

"Thank God."

"My sentiments exactly, sir."

"How did it happen, Agent Steele? Aren't the military police patrolling the housing areas? I've got a brigade of soldiers over here fighting to ensure that our world remains safe. Their families need to be protected, yet a killer gets on post and attacks my S-3's wife."

"Sir, we'll use every resource available to apprehend the perpetrator and bring him to justice."

"I want more than that. I want your assurance no one else will be injured."

"That's our goal, sir."

The colonel let out a sigh. "I know you're not to blame, but it's hard to believe something like this could have occurred."

Jamison filled him in on the few remaining details he knew, although he didn't mention his concern about Greg Yates and his wife's rumored infidelity. That could wait until the CID had more information.

"How's Roberta taking it?" the colonel asked.

"As well as can be expected, sir. She wants to speak to you." Jamison glanced at Michele before handing the phone to Mrs. Logan.

"I'm fine, Stanley," she said immediately.

Jamison left the kitchen. Major Bret Hansen, the medical examiner, had arrived and was examining the body. The major looked up as Jamison entered the living room.

"Appears the perp used neuromuscular incapacitation to subdue her," Hansen said.

"A stun gun?"

"More than likely."

"That explains how he got in. Mrs. Hughes probably thought one of the wives had arrived early when she opened the door. The killer incapacitated her with the stun gun and was able to walk in without confrontation."

"I'll do the autopsy in the morning and let you know the results."

"Sounds good, sir."

Returning to the kitchen, Jamison caught Mrs. Logan's eye. She raised her hand as if ready to finish her conversation.

"Erica should be able to keep the children until Yolanda's sister arrives. Have Curtis call me when he feels like talking." Mrs. Logan nodded. "I love you, too, dear."

Handing the phone to Michele, she said, "Your father wants to speak to you."

Taking the cell from her mother, Michele walked to the corner of the kitchen to talk privately with her father.

Jamison helped Mrs. Logan to her feet.

"I'm sure Stan's telling our daughter to take me home and keep me there. The man has enough to do without being concerned about my safety."

"He loves you, ma'am."

She nodded. "I'm lucky, Jamison. God gave me a wonderful husband and a good daughter, although she has an independent streak that worries me at times."

"She knows what she wants."

Mrs. Logan cocked her head and stared up at Jamison. "I'm not so sure about that."

Hearing noise outside, Jamison headed to the front of the house. Opening the door, he saw three women standing on the sidewalk, their faces twisted in disbelief.

"Excuse me, Jamison. Those are some of the brigade wives." Mrs. Logan shoved past him onto the porch. Pulling up the crime scene tape, she hurried toward the women.

Knowing her determination and desire to help the others, Jamison let her go. Any questions he still needed answered could wait.

Michele stepped onto the porch and handed him the phone. Her blue eyes had lost their brilliance, but they still had the power to draw him in just as they had done the first night they'd met at the club on post.

He turned from her, remembering the bitter taste of betrayal when Michele had left without explaining why. Usually he wasn't prone to hold a grudge, but in this case, he couldn't get past the sting of rejection. Maybe if she had told him what he had done wrong, Jamison might have been able to move on.

A beige van bearing the post maintenance company's logo pulled into the cul-de-sac. A tall, lanky fellow, mid-forties, eased to the pavement, toting a toolbox and a flashlight. "Someone called in an emergency request?"

One of the military policemen motioned for him to follow. "Right this way."

The tall guy smiled at Jamison. "Sir." His gaze took in Michele. "Evening, ma'am."

She nodded and, once again, wrapped her arms across her chest.

Extricating Mrs. Logan from the other brigade wives took longer than Jamison had expected. The women huddled around her like chicks surrounding a mother hen. She tried to assuage their fears, while Jamison cautioned them to remain vigilant until the killer was apprehended.

Michele knew most of the women and seemed as much a part of the group as her mother. She had the makings of a good army wife. Not that she seemed interested in marrying into the military. Her hasty departure from Fort Rickman had been ample proof she wanted nothing to do with Jamison or the army.

When the questioning had been completed and all the wives had left the area, Jamison drove Michele and her mother back to their home. A military policeman followed in Jamison's car.

"We're increasing patrols, especially in the housing areas, Mrs. Logan. I don't want to alarm you, but as I told the other women, you need to be careful and cautious."

"We will be, Jamison."

"Did you hear from Greg Yates? I didn't see him tonight."

Mrs. Logan checked her phone. "He didn't call. Maybe the weather kept him away."

Maybe. Or maybe not.

After saying good-night, Mrs. Logan hurried inside, leaving Michele to linger on the front steps. Gazing down at the cement, she chewed her lower lip.

Finally, she glanced up. "Thanks for responding to my call for help."

Jamison gave her a halfhearted smile that revealed nothing. "It's my job."

"Right." She looked away but not fast enough to hide the frown that tightened her brow.

He glanced at the street where the military policeman had parked his car. Memories of other times they had said good-night on this very same porch flashed through his mind.

Pushing aside the thoughts, Jamison squared his shoulders. "You had best get inside. Be sure to lock the door behind you."

She let out a frustrated breath. "Can't we, at least, go back to first names?"

"All right." He waited to see if she had anything else to say.

Michele tapped her hand against the wrought-iron banister and stared into the darkness, the silence heavy between them.

Finally, she broke the standoff. "How many military policemen will be in the area, Jamison?"

Her need for reassurance touched a chord in his heart. "Enough to keep you safe."

"I guess—" She raised her chin and regarded him with questioning eyes. "That's all we have to discuss."

"Michele—"

Before he could say anything else, she opened the front door. "Good night, Jamison."

The door closed, and the lock clicked into place.

If only we could go back in time. The thought came unbidden. Jamison slammed his fist into the palm of his other hand to dispel the temptation.

He was finished with Michele. End of story. Going back would only cause more pain.

Jamison double-timed back to his car, slid behind the wheel and pulled onto the roadway. He needed to distance himself from the colonel's daughter.

He had been hurt once.

Michele would never break his heart again.

TWO

Post security was imperative when a killer was on the loose. Jamison drove around Fort Rickman to ensure that the roadblocks were in place and the gates were well guarded. Heading back to his office, he realized, too late, that he had passed the turnoff to the CID headquarters and ended up in the area where the ranking officers lived.

The large brick quarters, built in the 1930s and '40s, circled a parade field where units marched and bands played in better times. Tonight the post was locked down and on high alert.

His headlights cut through the foggy darkness, revealing the two-lane street littered with fallen leaves and branches stripped from the trees during the earlier storms. Had the murderer chosen tonight because of the adverse weather conditions, or had something else triggered his assault?

At the onset of any investigation, Jamison felt like a man in a rowboat, paddling through uncharted waters in the middle of a black night, never knowing where his journey would end. The fog lifted momentarily, revealing the Logans' quarters.

Jamison almost smiled. He didn't need to check on Michele. Military police were patrolling the colonel's area.

They were trained and competent, but for some reason, his radar had signaled the need to ensure that Michele was safe.

The front porch light was on and mixed with the glow from a lamp in the living room. Upstairs, a single bulb shone through a bathroom window. Slowing his speed, he studied the area around the house, looking for anything that could signal danger for the women inside. Extending his search, he checked the entire block before he returned to her street.

A military police patrol car approached from the opposite direction. Not wanting to explain why he was in the area, Jamison turned at the next intersection and headed back to CID headquarters.

Along the way, he tried to convince himself that he would have done the same thing no matter who had been a witness in the investigation. Deep down, he knew the truth. Michele had been the only reason for his late-night detour.

Once behind his desk, Jamison placed a call to the CID in Afghanistan and filled them in on what had happened at Fort Rickman. A special agent by the name of Warner took the information and assured Jamison he'd see what he could uncover about Major Shirley Yates. If she had previously had a romantic relationship or was currently having an affair, Warner would find out who was involved and contact Jamison with the information. He would also check out Major Hughes to ensure that the murder wasn't an act of revenge against the victim's husband.

For the rest of the night, Jamison pored over the crime scene photos and information collected so far. By morning, his shoulders ached. He scooted his chair back and picked up a photo taken of the Hughes' kitchen and the door through which the killer had escaped.

In the corner of the same picture, the photographer

had also captured Michele, standing by the table, arms wrapped across her chest. The look on her face provided a clear image of the turmoil she must have been experiencing internally. The shock of finding a murder victim was hard on anyone, especially so for a woman who ran from conflict. Michele might consider herself strong and determined, but Jamison knew better.

They had met a little over a year after the helicopter crash that had taken her brother's life. Michele worked with insurance actuary tables and knew the dangers those in the military faced, especially when deployed or training for combat. A job with the CID brought danger even closer to home, something she wasn't willing to face.

Ten months ago, Michele had run away from a relationship that would have required her to look deep within herself and determine whether she cared enough about Jamison to live with the constant threat a job in law enforcement entailed.

Since she had never told him why she had moved back to Atlanta, Jamison had been left with two possible conclusions. Michele had decided he wasn't worth the risk or she hadn't been able to determine what she wanted in life.

On occasion, she had mentioned her struggle with God. If she didn't feel loved by the Lord, chances were she didn't feel worthy of anyone's love, including Jamison's. Either way, she had run to Atlanta, where she thought she could live life on her own terms. Her own safe terms.

Love involved risk, and Michele wasn't ready to put her heart on the line. At least, that's the excuse Jamison had used to work through his own pain. He thought he had healed, but coming face-to-face with Michele made him realize he wasn't over her yet. For some reason—maybe lack of sleep or the horrific crime scene that had been captured in the photos on his desk—Jamison felt raw as if being near Michele had opened the old wound to his heart.

Tossing the picture of her back onto his desk, he looked up as Dawson entered the cubicle with two steaming mugs of coffee in hand.

"Otis perked a fresh pot," Dawson said in greeting.

"God bless him." Jamison reached for a mug and inhaled the rich aroma.

Dawson's gaze trailed over Jamison's desk and stopped at the photo of Michele. Inwardly, Jamison flinched, waiting for a jabbing comment about a pretty face and a former love.

Relieved when the other CID agent raised his gaze without commenting, Jamison asked, "What about the door-to-door search in the neighborhood? Anything turn up yet?"

"Only questions about the maintenance man who fixed the wiring at the Hughes quarters last night."

"The guy from Prime Maintenance?" Jamison took a swig of the hot brew. High-test, loaded with caffeine, just what he needed after a long night without sleep.

Dawson nodded. "A couple folks mentioned seeing his truck drive through the housing area earlier in the evening."

"Their main office isn't far from the Post Shopping Area. I'll stop by and talk to the supervisor." Jamison straightened the stack of photos on his desk and pulled out an eight-by-ten of Yolanda's dining room. He tapped his finger on the bouquet of cut flowers in the center of the table. "The crime scene team found a floral wrapper from the post flower shop in the victim's trash. I plan to question the florist, as well, after I shower and change. He may have seen something when he delivered the bouquet."

"Let me know what you find out."

"Will do." Jamison took another sip of his coffee. "Send

one of our guys into Freemont to talk to Mr. Yates. We need to know why he never showed up at the potluck last night. And keep an extra detail of military police on the front gate. Every vehicle leaving and entering Fort Rickman needs to be searched. If the killer got away last night, we don't want him coming back on post and doing more harm."

"You worried he'll strike again?" Dawson asked.

"Aren't you?"

The other agent shrugged. "Maybe I'm being optimistic, but knife wounds are personal, which is what I keep thinking this crime was. The perp knew Yolanda Hughes. He wanted to kill her for some reason we need to determine. Maybe it involved a love triangle or maybe it was something else and she's his only intended victim. Once we learn his motive, we'll be able to track him down."

"And if he kills again before we find him?"

"Then I'll have to admit I was wrong." He stared at Jamison for a long moment. The memory of walking into the ambush ten months ago hung between them.

Jamison still felt responsible. "Look, Dawson—"

As much as he wanted to clear up what had happened, the words stuck in his throat. Instead of his own voice, he heard his father's taunts about his inability to do anything right. "Jamie-boy, you're a failure," replayed over and over in his mind. Not that anything his father said should have bearing on his life today.

Frustrated that the long-ago censure still affected him, Jamison let out a lungful of air and placed his cup on his desk. "After I shower at the gym, I'll talk to the maintenance company and the florist. Call me if anything new surfaces."

When he left the gym, Jamison planned to stop by the maintenance office, but just as last night, he ended up in front of Colonel Logan's quarters. A number of cars were parked at the curb. Jamison hustled up the steps and rang the bell. Mrs. Logan answered the door. Women's voices sounded from the living room.

"Morning, ma'am. I wanted to ensure that you and Michele had an uneventful night and are doing okay." He peered around her to the women inside, recognizing many of the wives who had gathered at the Hughes residence last night.

"We're fine, Jamison, but it's nice of you to stop by and inquire about our well-being. Michele's right here—"

Mrs. Logan stepped away from the door.

"Ah, ma'am—"

He didn't need to talk to Michele.

"Jamison?" Dressed in a pretty floral blouse and cotton slacks, Michele appeared in the doorway, looking like a summer garden.

Internally, he groaned. "I was just checking to see if you're all right."

"Yes, of course." Her lips smiled, but her eyes remained guarded. "The military police are patrolling our area and keeping us safe."

Her tone caused him to bristle. *Note to self, Michele doesn't need you in her life.*

"Sounds like you've got a full house."

"The wives wanted to be together. They're worried and grieving and ready for their husbands to return home." She stepped onto the porch and pulled the door closed behind her. "How's the investigation going?"

"We don't have much at this point. A few people to question. We're checking everyone coming on and off post and have enhanced security in all the housing areas."

"I noticed the military police driving by a number of times last night."

From the look on her face, Jamison wondered if she had seen his car. He cleared his throat, trying to ignore the smoothness of her cheeks and the way her hair gleamed in the morning light. "Any word on the Hughes children?"

"Their dad plans to talk to them tonight on Skype." Her voice softened and sadness tugged at the corners of her mouth.

Jamison's heart ached for the children. His own mother had died when he was young, and he knew how hard life could be for kids without a mom.

"I made chocolate chip cookies and took them over early this morning. Yolanda's sister is scheduled to arrive later today. She and the kids will stay in the VIP guest quarters until Major Hughes arrives home."

"Any idea about the burial?"

"They have a plot in Missouri. Once everyone is re-united, Major Hughes and the children will fly her body home. Mother and Dad will probably attend the funeral. I'm not sure what I should do."

Knowing Michele, she would probably run back to Atlanta. Just as she had done ten months ago.

He glanced at his watch, needing to distance himself from the colonel's daughter. "You have my number. Call if you need anything."

"Thank you, Jamison."

He hurried back to his car. Five minutes with Michele and suddenly his ordered life was anything but. His focus needed to center on the investigation and the supervisor at Prime Maintenance he planned to question, as well as the florist on post.

Pulling away from the Logan quarters, Jamison shook his head, frustrated with the swell of feelings that were bubbling up within him.

A woman murdered.

A killer on the loose.

A very personal complication he hadn't expected that tangled up his ability to be objective.

"Oh, Michele," he groaned aloud. "Why'd you have to come back to Fort Rickman now?"

Traffic was light as Michele drove across post. The gray sky and the weather forecaster's prediction that another round of turbulence would hit the area added to her unease.

Over the last few hours, Michele's mood had dropped as low as the barometer. She needed time away from her mother and the women who filled the Logan home. Sweet as they were, their long faces and hushed tones as they spoke of what had happened forced her to confront the terrible tragedy she had stumbled upon last night.

Knowing two children had been left without a mother added to her struggle. Seeing their sweet faces earlier in the day had put an even heavier pall around her shoulders. Michele needed fresh air and time to process her emotions, but no matter how hard she tried to block the crime scene from her memory, the gruesome pictures of Yolanda's death continued to haunt her.

The expression on Jamison's face when he had come crashing into the house, gun in hand, mixed with the other still frames. Ten months ago, she had thought she loved him, but when an investigation almost claimed his life, she realized her mistake. Maybe in time, she'd find Mr. Right. At the moment, she was more concerned about her confrontation last night with Mr. Wrong. Seeing him again this morning had added more confusion to the day.

Despite his good qualities, Jamison wasn't the man for her. Everything inside her warned that a U.S. Army warrant officer, who was also a CID special agent, was off-limits and could end up being a deadly combination. Plus, her recent history with the military wasn't good.

In quick flashes, she thought of her brother's death, her father's injury soon after he arrived in Afghanistan and the shoot-out on post that could have left Jamison wounded. Or dead.

Dawson had taken the bullet meant for Jamison. In spite of the close call, Jamison continued to handle investigations that put him in danger, which further proved the CID agent wasn't for her.

So why had she called him yesterday? Jamison, of all people. She'd reacted without thinking. Now she had to pay the price for seeing him again.

Last night, he had been cool, calm and totally in control, dressed in a starched white shirt, a silk tie and a sports coat expertly tailored to fit his broad shoulders and trim waist.

Instead of a military uniform, CID agents wore civilian clothes to ensure that rank didn't get in the way of their investigations. Maybe that's what had attracted her to Jamison the night they'd met at the military club on post. He had looked drop-dead gorgeous in his coat and tie when he extended his hand in greeting, along with a smile that instantly melted her heart.

Slipping her right hand into his and gazing into his deep-set brown eyes had made her world stop for one breathless moment. Something had clicked inside her, and she had been instantly smitten by the very special, special agent.

He'd been equally put together last night, although his eyes had been darker than she remembered. Probably because he had refused to hold her gaze, which bothered her more than she wanted to admit. This morning he'd seemed a bit on edge, although it was no wonder after what had happened.

Anyone who didn't know him wouldn't notice the tiny lines around his eyes or the fatigue that played over his features. Committed as he had always been to his job, he had probably slept little last night.

Heaving a sigh, she turned into the main shopping area on post and parked across from the floral shop. A bell tinkled over the door as she entered the air-conditioned interior and stepped toward the counter.

The florist, in his early forties and with a muscular build and military flattop, glanced up. "May I help you?"

"I called in an order last week for a bouquet of cut flowers."

"Name?"

"Logan. Michele Logan."

Recognition played over his angled face. "You're Colonel Logan's daughter."

"That's right."

"I served with your dad in Iraq when he was a battalion commander. Best commander I ever had."

Michele never tired of hearing good things about her father. Three years ago, after bringing his battalion of soldiers home from Iraq, her dad had been promoted to full colonel and selected for brigade command. Some said he was a shoo-in for general officer. Not that he allowed praise to impact the way he did his job.

Their family's only dark moment during that time had been Lance's death. A helicopter crash shortly after her brother had graduated from flight school and moved to his new military assignment at Fort Knox, Kentucky. A freak accident that never should have happened.

The hardest part was knowing she could have prevented the tragedy. Lance wouldn't have been flying if Michele had accepted his invitation to visit him that weekend. She had made the wrong decision, a decision that led to her brother's death.

Unable to work through her grief and her guilt, Michele had eventually buried her pain. Finding Yolanda yesterday had brought everything to the surface.

The florist stretched out his hand. "Name's Teddy Sutherland."

Michele returned the handshake, noting his firm grip and thick, stubby fingers. "Nice to meet you, sir."

"I've got your order. You said you wanted a container appropriate for your brother's grave site?"

"That's right." She momentarily averted her gaze, blinking back unexpected tears that flooded her eyes. Her emotions hovered close to the surface today.

Teddy flipped through a stack of order forms. "I remember hearing about the helicopter crash. Wasn't your brother the only one on board who died?"

She nodded, wondering yet again about the inequity of the accident. Not that she had wanted anyone else to lose a loved one in the crash. She just didn't understand why her brother had to die.

"About this time of year, as I recall?"

The florist's concern touched her. She nodded, her voice halting when she spoke. "It…it happened two years ago today."

"Tough on your mom, no doubt, especially after last night."

"You heard about the murder?"

"News travels fast on post. Wonder if they'll ever find the guy." He reached into the large walk-in refrigerator and pulled out a bouquet of red gladiolas and white mums arranged with miniature American flags and wrapped together with a blue ribbon.

Placing the flowers on the counter along with a plastic

vase and a small attachment to anchor the arrangement into the ground, the florist glanced up, waiting for her reaction.

"They're beautiful, Mr. Sutherland."

"It's Teddy, please. Tell your mother I'm ordering flowers for the welcome-home ceremony."

"To give to the wives in the brigade?"

He nodded. "Mrs. Grayson, the executive officer's wife, asked me to help." He glanced down, somewhat embarrassed by his gesture. "The way I feel about your dad, it's the least I could do."

"I know my mother and the other wives will appreciate your generosity."

The bell over the door tinkled. Michele turned, expecting to see another customer. Her breath caught in her throat as Jamison entered the store.

She smiled, trying to override the tension that wrapped around her as tightly as the wire holding the floral bow in place. He nodded, then glanced away for a moment in an obvious attempt to cover his own unease.

Turning back to the flowers, Michele fiddled with the ribbon.

Jamison stepped closer and touched the plastic vase lying on the counter. "Two years ago, wasn't it, Michele?"

She hadn't expected him to remember. The empathy she heard in his voice caused her eyes to cloud again. Jamison had understood when no one else seemed interested in how a younger sister felt about the death of the brother she idolized. Even her parents hadn't wanted to talk about their son's future cut short.

Teddy swiped her credit card and ripped off the tape register receipt. Holding out the thin strip of paper, he handed Michele a pen. "I just need a signature to complete the transaction."

Relieved to focus on something other than the special

agent, Michele hastily signed her name. Grabbing the flowers and vase, she turned to find Jamison standing much too close.

She dropped her gaze, trying to ignore his muscular shoulders and the manly scent of his aftershave. Instead her focus settled on his right hip, where—beneath the smooth line of his sports coat—he carried a SIG Sauer, loaded and ready to fire.

"Sorry." He stepped aside. His demeanor and voice, now devoid of inflection, reminded her that their involvement had ended months ago. Just as with Lance, she had no reason to think about what might have been.

Ironically, on her brother's last trip home, Lance had laughingly teased that only a military guy would make her happy. Michele had agreed, but his death had changed her mind. Now she just wanted to guard her future and her heart.

The bell tinkled as she pushed the door open and stepped into the Georgia humidity, grateful no one was standing close enough to see the confusion she couldn't hide and shouldn't be feeling. She'd left Jamison months ago. A good decision, or so she'd thought.

Slipping behind the wheel of her car, she glanced back at the florist shop. Would she have felt differently if her brother hadn't died?

Maybe then she wouldn't have been afraid of her feelings for the CID agent. But Lance *had* died and her father had been injured in Afghanistan, and then Dawson had taken a bullet meant for Jamison in a bloody shoot-out that had made her run scared.

Now Yolanda.

If only Michele could run away again, just as she had done ten months ago. She wanted to go back to the secure life she'd made for herself in Atlanta, but she couldn't leave her mother alone after the tragedy that had happened. The brigade would return sometime next week. Michele would wait until her father came home before she left Fort Rickman and the military.

By then, Jamison would have found the killer.

Her stomach tightened and a gasp escaped her lips as she realized that finding the killer would, once again, put Jamison in the line of fire.

Why did Michele continue to get under his skin?

Jamison clamped down on his jaw and pulled in a deep breath, needing to distance himself, at least emotionally, from the colonel's daughter and concentrate on the florist, who continued to stare at him.

"Can I help you, sir?" he asked a second time.

Glancing at the clerk's name tag, Jamison held up his CID identification. "I need information about any floral deliveries you've made in the last couple days, Mr. Sutherland."

The florist nodded. "You're here because of that murder on post."

A crime everyone seemed to have heard about by now. "What can you tell me?"

"Mrs. Hughes ordered a bouquet for yesterday afternoon." Sutherland flipped through his order forms. "Here it is. A bouquet of cut flowers, carnations and daisies, interspersed with a few yellow roses."

Glancing up at Jamison, he added, "Yellow roses are a popular homecoming flower. As you probably know, Major Hughes's unit is scheduled to return to Fort Rickman next week."

"Did Mrs. Hughes discuss her husband's return to post?"

The florist shook his head. "Not to me, but it's common

knowledge. Plus, the local chamber of commerce keeps track of all the homecomings. Having the brigade back will be good for business."

Jamison pulled his notebook and pen from his pocket. "What time did you deliver the flowers to the Hughes residence?"

"I didn't. Mrs. Hughes stopped by the shop yesterday and placed the order before she went to the commissary. I had the table arrangement ready when she finished shopping."

"Did she say why she wanted flowers?"

"No, sir, but Mrs. Hughes bought flowers once a month or so. Usually for a wives' event. Sure is a shame."

"How'd you learn about her death?"

"One of her neighbors stopped in earlier today. She was pretty shook-up. Fact is everyone's upset."

"Do you recall the neighbor's name?"

"I can find it if you give me a minute." Once again, he sorted through the order forms. His face lit up as he pulled a paper from the pile and held it out to Jamison. "Ursula Barker bought an arrangement shortly after I opened this morning. She lives down the street from the Hugheses and shared that the whole neighborhood is worried. Course, I don't blame them with a killer on the loose. I'm worried, too. You guys have any idea who did it?"

"I'm not at liberty to say." A pat answer, but the truth was that the CID and military police had nothing concrete to go on so far.

The florist pursed his lips. "Guess I shouldn't have asked, but just like everyone else on post, I'm looking over my shoulder, if you know what I mean."

Jamison did know. No one wanted a murderer on the loose. He continued to question the florist but learned nothing more that would have a bearing on the victim's death. After leaving the floral shop, Jamison called CID headquarters. He quickly filled Dawson in on his interview with the florist before he turned the discussion to his earlier stop at Prime Maintenance.

"I talked to the supervisor. The only maintenance man on duty last night was Danny Altman. He's prior military, worked in Atlanta and was questioned when his girlfriend died unexpectedly. Her death was ruled accidental." Jamison passed on Altman's Freemont address. "Find out more about the girlfriend."

"Roger that. I'll talk to Mr. Altman and see if he remembers anything pertinent concerning last night, as well." Dawson paused for a long moment. "I talked to McGrunner."

Both Dawson and Jamison thought highly of the young military policeman who had a good work ethic and the makings of a future CID special agent. He had been on patrol last night, and Jamison knew where Dawson was headed.

"Look, Dawson, I drove by Colonel Logan's quarters," Jamison admitted. "That's all."

"Military police were on patrol in the colonel's housing area. You didn't need to worry about Michele."

"The killer left two witnesses behind."

"Yes, but neither Michele nor her mother can identify him."

"He may not realize that. If I were a killer, I'd get rid of everyone involved." The muscles in Jamison's neck tensed as he thought about what could happen. "Did any of the neighbors hear sounds of a struggle?"

"Negative."

"I blame that on the storm. Most folks were probably hunkered down inside their quarters. Thunder and wind would have muffled any noise coming from the victim's quarters."

"Roger that," Dawson agreed. "And if the killer had used a stun gun, Mrs. Hughes would have quickly lost muscle control and couldn't have screamed for help."

What about Michele? The thought of her with the killer made Jamison clamp down on his jaw.

Thank God she and Mrs. Logan hadn't been hurt.

He pushed the cell closer to his ear. "Any word from the medical examiner?"

"Negative."

Seemed they were still batting zero. Although it might be a long shot, Jamison thought of another person who needed to be questioned. "The florist said a neighbor by the name of Ursula Barker told him about the victim's death. Have one of our people check with Ms. Barker and verify the florist's story."

"You think he's lying?"

"I just want to be sure."

Dawson was quiet for a long moment. "You're still stalled because of the last case we worked on together."

"I told you, I'm okay."

"You can trust your instincts, buddy. Whatever you think you did wrong—"

Jamison let out a blast of pent-up air. "Dawson."

"Seeing Michele yesterday…" The CID agent sighed. "I know how you felt about her."

"It's over, Dawson. End of discussion."

"Yeah, right."

"Don't forget Ursula Barker. Then get back to me."

Frustrated, Jamison disconnected and hustled to his car. His mind relived visions of when Dawson had taken the hit meant for Jamison. Fast-forward to yesterday and what could have happened to Michele.

Climbing behind the wheel, he started the ignition and pulled out of the parking lot. At one time, his instincts had been good, but he and Dawson had walked into an ambush any rookie cop could have seen coming. Now he had to check and double-check his actions to keep from making another mistake.

Dark clouds billowed in the sky overhead, and a strong gust of wind tugged at his car. Gripping the steering wheel, Jamison eyed the rapidly worsening weather.

What had he missed last night? Mrs. Logan and Michele hadn't provided information that could identify the killer, but just as he'd told Dawson, if the perpetrator thought they could ID him, wouldn't he come after them?

Jamison called Dawson back. "Increase surveillance around Colonel Logan's quarters."

"Did something happen?"

"Not yet, but I want to make sure it doesn't."

Disconnecting, he increased his speed.

Michele was driving along narrow back roads with a storm rolling into the area. More threatening than the weather was the out-of-the-way location of the cemetery, where she would be alone and at risk. This time, he didn't need to double-check the facts.

Michele was vulnerable and unprotected.

Every instinct warned Jamison to hurry.

THREE

Michele drummed her hand on the steering wheel as she sat in the line of cars snaking their way through the Main Gate. Up ahead a military policeman worked with two civilian gate guards, checking the vehicles leaving post.

Across the median, a swarm of MPs searched the interior—as well as under the hood and in the trunk—of every car entering the garrison. Trucks were subject to more detailed scrutiny. With Fort Rickman on lockdown, law enforcement was ensuring that no one brought anything suspicious on or off post without their knowledge.

Though she was reassured by the thoroughness of the military police, Michele was frustrated by the delay. Her eyes turned upward, taking in the darkening sky and the wind that picked through the Spanish moss hanging from the stately oaks that lined the side of the road. If she didn't reach the cemetery soon, she could get caught in a downpour.

The whole post was on edge, and rightfully so. Anyone with a smattering of knowledge about army operations could easily learn the names of the deployed soldiers. A quick search of a Fort Rickman phone book would provide home addresses where family members would be easy targets.

Had Yolanda been a random victim? Or was she chosen because her husband was deployed and she was alone?

A number of times last night, Michele had heard cars driving by outside. Looking from her bedroom window, she'd seen a steady stream of military police sedans patrolling the area. The added protection should have made her feel more secure but only drove home the fact that a killer was on the loose. The only time she'd felt safe was when Jamison was with her. But his presence created its own set of problems.

Michele rubbed her hand over her stomach in an attempt to quell the nervous confusion eating at her. She needed to push thoughts of him aside and concentrate on getting to the cemetery before the next round of storms.

The line of traffic moved forward. Michele edged her car toward the gate and stopped in front of the guard. He glanced into the interior of her vehicle and then checked her trunk before he waved her on.

As she left the post, she passed three media vans parked in a clearing at the side of the road. Camera crews stood in a huddle, no doubt eager to broadcast the latest news about Yolanda's death.

Once she was on Freemont Road, Michele increased her speed and after a series of turns spied the front entrance to the cemetery up ahead. Putting on her signal, she turned onto the narrow road, full of twists and turns, that meandered through the sprawling grounds of gentle knolls and stands of trees.

Lance had loved the outdoors, and her parents had chosen a secluded burial plot atop a small rise that provided a clear view of the surrounding grounds. Michele parked on the grass just short of the rise.

As a precaution and noting the recent drop in temperature, she grabbed a raincoat off the backseat and, with her purse and flowers in hand, trudged up the incline. The ground, still damp from last night's rain, cushioned her footfalls.

Over her right shoulder, she noticed a car parked near a cluster of monuments shaded by a giant oak tree. A man stood nearby. As she watched, he raised binoculars to his eyes and stared in her direction.

The hair on the back of her neck tingled. Unable to ignore the warning, she shivered, not from the wind that whipped around her but from her own nervousness. Lightning danced across the sky followed by the rumble of thunder.

Thankful for the waterproof slicker, Michele shrugged into the thick vinyl and pulled her hair free from the neck of the coat. She felt violated by the man's prying gaze and wrapped the coat across her chest as she hurried on to the crest of the hill.

Once there, she glanced back, relieved to see that the man with the binoculars had climbed into his car to leave the cemetery. Turning her thoughts to Lance, she approached the rear of his monument.

Instead of a small and simple military marker, her parents had chosen a larger memorial with Lance's picture etched into the front of the stone. As a template for his likeness, they had used a photograph Michele had taken at his graduation from flight school.

She and her parents had attended the ceremony at Fort Rucker, Alabama, and had been so proud of Lance, standing tall in his uniform in front of the American flag he loved. Three months later, his chopper crashed and exploded into a flaming inferno that took his life.

Stopped by the painful memory, Michele touched the cool granite. "Oh, Lance," she sighed, wishing she weren't alone with her grief. Her mother never came with her, never even wanted to, which Michele didn't understand.

She thought of Jamison. Would he have accepted her invitation if she had asked him? Probably not. He had a murder to solve.

From out of nowhere, the smell of blood wafted past her. Yolanda's bleeding body swam before her eyes. Michele bristled, annoyed with the tricks her mind was playing.

Struggling to shrug off the frightful memory, she rounded the monument and peered down, expecting to find her brother's likeness smiling up at her.

At first unable to comprehend what she was seeing, Michele leaned closer. Then, like an arrow to her heart, realization hit.

She gasped. The flowers dropped to the rain-dampened earth. Lightning ripped across the sky. Seconds later, thunder mixed with the roar of her pounding pulse.

Vandals had chiseled thick gashes into Lance's image, turning his handsome countenance into a macabre caricature. The marks cut into the stone exactly where the killer's knife had slashed Yolanda's flesh. A dark, viscous substance covered the mutilation and dripped like blood over his name and the date of his death.

Unable to look any longer at the defacement, Michele turned and ran away. Down the hill she fled, trying to distance herself from the desecration of her brother's grave. Fat raindrops pummeled her face and mixed with the tears cascading down her cheeks.

She skidded. Her feet slipped on the wet grass. Stumbling, she righted herself and hurried on. Michele reached the road on the opposite side of a sharp curve from where she had parked her car.

The sky opened up as if it, too, were weeping for the dead. She dug in her purse, searching for her keys, and raced around the bend, hardly able to see because of the tears flooding her eyes.

The sound of tires rolling over asphalt startled her. She glanced up. Her heart jammed in her throat.

A car loomed in front of her.

Black sedan, tinted windows. The chrome hood ornament was headed straight for her.

She lunged, trying to jump clear.

The fender and outer side panel swiped against her thigh and sent her flying like a rag doll. Hot streaks of pain ricocheted through her body. She fell to the ground, clutching her leg and gasping for breath.

Unable to cry for help, Michele lay in pouring rain enveloped by darkness.

Jamison's heart stopped as he pulled into the cemetery. In one terrifying flash, he saw it all play out.

Michele!

Accelerating, he raced forward, taking the turns at breakneck speed. *Please, God, let her be okay.*

Punching Speed Dial on his cell, he connected with the local police. "Hit-and-run at the Freemont Cemetery. Send an ambulance and police. *Now!*"

Fear clamped down on his gut. Would he get to her in time?

Halfway into the last curve, the tires lost traction. Jamison eased up on the accelerator and turned the wheel into the skid. Once the car had straightened, he put his foot on the gas and closed the distance to where she lay.

Leaping from his car, he charged across the rain-sloshed grass. His only thought was Michele.

Fingers of dread clawed at his throat. The rain eased as he dropped to his knees beside her.

"Michele, it's Jamison. Talk to me."

Water-drenched hair covered her face. He pushed away the wayward strands. Her skin was pale, too pale.

Please, God!

Long lashes moved ever so slightly, fanning her cheeks.

He touched her neck, feeling a steady pulse, and gasped with relief.

She jerked at his touch.

"It's okay, honey. An ambulance is on the way."

Sirens screamed in the distance.

"Open your eyes, Michele."

She groaned. Her lashes fluttered, revealing cornflower-blue orbs clouded with confusion.

"You're going to be all right. There's nothing to worry about." As he tried to comfort her, Jamison worked his hands over her arms and lower legs, ensuring that none of her bones had been broken.

She flinched when he gently prodded her knee, probably where she had taken the greatest impact from the hit.

Anger surged through him at the maniac who had done this to her and then had driven away, never checking to ensure that she was still alive. Jamison wanted to pound his fist into the wet earth at his own stupidity. He shouldn't have let her leave the floral shop alone.

"La...Lance's grave site." She tried to sit up.

He gently touched her shoulder. "Lie still until the EMTs arrive."

She grabbed his hand. "The m...monument was desecrated."

Sirens filled the air. Two Freemont police cars pulled into the cemetery and stopped close to where Michele lay. An ambulance turned onto the grounds. Overcome with relief, Jamison remained at her side as the officers neared.

The older of the two made the introductions. "Sir, I'm Officer Tim Simpson with the Freemont Police Department." Mid-forties, the guy had a buzz cut and thick brows that he raised as he pointed to the wiry, younger officer next to him. "This is Officer Bobby Jones."

Jamison flashed his identification, gave his own name and Michele's and quickly explained what he had witnessed.

"I saw Miss Logan when I pulled into the cemetery. She was hurrying around the curve in the road toward her car. The rain was falling hard, and she was trying to pull her cell phone or her keys from her handbag."

"M…my keys," she responded, her voice weak.

"The car appeared to accelerate just before it hit her," Jamison added.

She glanced at Simpson. "I…I didn't hear a motor."

"Can you give us a description of the vehicle, ma'am?"

"Black or dark blue with a silver hood ornament." She shook her head. "I'm not sure about the make or model."

"Were you able to see the driver?" Jamison asked, still hovering over her.

"The windows were tinted. Earlier, a man…by the oak tree. He had binoculars."

"Military binoculars?"

"I'm not sure. I thought he'd left the cemetery by the front entrance." She wrinkled her brow. "It could have been the same car."

The cop looked at Jamison. "Did you get a visual, sir?"

"Not on the driver. I was too far away, and he left through the rear exit. The vehicle was a small, four-door sedan with tinted windows, as Miss Logan mentioned. Late model. Dark color. Could have been a hybrid."

Simpson pursed his lips. "Which would have been the reason she didn't hear the engine."

"Exactly."

The ambulance pulled alongside the police cars, and

two EMTs quickly approached. "Sir, can you step back and give us some room?"

As much as Jamison didn't want to leave Michele's side, he had to let the medical team do their job.

He squeezed her hand. "I'll talk to the police while the EMTs ensure that you're okay."

Her grip tightened. "Lance's grave. Someone cut into his marker."

"I'm heading there now."

As the EMTs strapped Michele to a backboard, Jamison turned to Officer Jones. "Can you get the names off the headstones near the oak tree? The family members need to be questioned in case one of them was the man with binoculars."

"Good idea. I'll take care of it."

Jamison motioned to the older cop and then pointed up the incline. "Let's take a walk and check out the marker."

Having visited Lance's grave with Michele on occasion, Jamison led the way. His stomach soured at the sight of the damage done to the monument. What kind of vicious person would do such a hateful act?

Bending down, he studied the cuts in the granite and the spattered liquid. "Looks like blood, although it might not be human."

Simpson nodded. "A piece of raw steak could provide enough blood to cover the entire monument." He scratched off a sample and dropped it into a plastic evidence bag. "Whatever it is, I'll have it analyzed and let you know the results."

Jamison glanced back at where the EMTs were talking to Michele. A heavy weight settled on his shoulders.

The grave desecration was a vindictive act against the Logan family. Judging from the location of gash marks on Lance's etched likeness, the defacement appeared to be connected to the murder on post.

Jamison's heart lurched with a terrifying realization. The cold, hard truth sent chills along his spine. Just like with Dawson, Jamison hadn't put the pieces together fast enough to realize Michele would be an easy target at the cemetery. That mistake had almost cost Michele her life.

FOUR

As much as Michele didn't want to go to the hospital, she gave in at the insistence of the EMTs. Freemont had a modern facility with a good emergency room where she could be checked over by a physician.

"You're one lucky lady," the driver of the ambulance told her as the EMTs repacked their equipment and prepared to leave the cemetery.

Michele didn't feel lucky. Her thigh ached, and she must have pulled a muscle in her back when she landed on the rain-soaked grass. Nothing serious, she felt sure, but not what she wanted today, of all days.

Jamison stood away from the circle of first responders, cell phone jammed to his ear, as he relayed what had happened back to CID headquarters. She had warned him not to call her mother. Not yet, at least.

Roberta had enough to worry her without hearing her daughter was involved in a hit-and-run accident. Once the doctor at the hospital gave the all clear, Michele planned to call home with positive news that she was all right.

Disconnecting, Jamison approached the stretcher where she lay and touched her hand. His eyes were darker than usual, his brow drawn in what seemed like a continuous frown. Jamison had laughed so often when they were dating that she considered asking him to force a smile or, at least, relax the tension that tugged at his full lips.

She remembered how he used to tease her with his kisses. In the beginning, the warmth of his embrace and the sweet gentleness of his caresses had melted the cold interior of her heart, a heart that had frozen after Lance's death.

Jamison had been a good influence when they'd dated. His optimism had rubbed off on her. Without realizing it at the time, Michele had started to share his vision of how life was meant to be lived, in the present and with hope for the future.

After she left Fort Rickman, the light Jamison had brought into her life dimmed, leaving a noticeable void.

Jamison's love for life seemed to have diminished, as well. Could ten months have made such a significant difference in both of their lives?

Tragedy was transforming and not necessarily for the better. The shoot-out on post ten months ago could have been the catalyst that caused the change in Jamison. Or had something else been the reason?

Something or someone?

Unable to accept that she might be to blame for Jamison's newfound gloom, Michele fisted her hands.

Jamison leaned over the stretcher, his face so close she could feel his warm breath against her cheek. "What's wrong, Michele? Did you remember something?"

She remembered his kisses. "Did you tell Dawson not to call my mother?"

"I said you planned to notify her once you arrived at Freemont Hospital."

The EMT tapped Jamison's shoulder. "We're ready to transport."

He squeezed her hand and smiled, not only with his lips

but also with his eyes. For a brief moment, his gaze bathed her in a warmth that took away the chilling fear that had blanketed her for too long.

"You'll be with me at the hospital?" she asked, needing assurance he wouldn't leave her.

"Ah, sir," the medic interrupted. "You can drive your own vehicle and meet us at the E.R."

Releasing her hand, Jamison took a step toward the surprised EMT and jammed his finger into the guy's chest.

"Let's get this straight. I'm riding in the ambulance with the patient."

The medic's eyes widened for a moment before he shrugged. "Whatever you say, sir."

True to his word, Jamison hovered close to her side not only during the drive to the hospital, but also while she waited in the exam room to see the doctor. Once the physician appeared, Jamison moved into the hallway. He stood guard outside her door while the doctor completed his assessment and ordered a battery of laboratory tests and X-rays.

"You can come back in here," Michele said to Jamison through the half-opened door after the doc had moved on to the next patient.

"Thanks, but I'll stay put." Jamison's stance, his pursed lips and the tight pull on his square jaw were outward signs he was in full bodyguard mode. Had something else happened that had put him on high alert?

Before she had time to ask, an aide appeared and pushed her to X-ray. Jamison followed close behind the stretcher. His focused gaze swept the corridor. Every few seconds, he turned to scan the hallway behind them.

Surely he was being overly cautious. Although after Yolanda's death and her own run-in with the driver at the cemetery, Michele was relieved to have someone watching her back, a very stoic someone who said little and kept his facial expressions to a minimum.

A friendly tech x-rayed her legs and spinal column, after which Michele returned to the exam room. Just as before, Jamison remained in the hallway, eyeing the flow of medical personnel and patients.

"Did something happen?" Michele finally asked, no longer able to keep her curiosity in check.

Jamison leaned into her room. "While you were with the doc, one of the nurses mentioned some strange dudes in the waiting area."

Michele rolled her eyes. "Are you always on duty?"

His lips twitched ever so slightly before he returned to his guard post.

She glanced at her watch. What was taking so long? A few minutes later, she checked the time again. And then again.

Everything moved slowly in the emergency room, which frustrated Michele. She had told her mother she planned to run a few errands when she left the house earlier in the day. By now, Roberta would be worried something had happened.

Closing her eyes, Michele tried to stave off the growing anxiety and opened them seconds later to find Jamison next to her, cell phone in hand. "Time to call home."

"How…how did you know what I was thinking?"

"You kept checking your watch."

Her mother sounded relieved when she heard Michele's voice. Choosing her words carefully, Michele relayed what had happened in an upbeat, breezy way.

Of course, Roberta instantly picked up on Michele's attempt to soft-pedal the news. Before she could completely reassure her mother, a lab tech appeared, needing one more vial of blood.

"Don't say anything to worry her," Michele mouthed as she passed the phone to Jamison and then fisted her hand for the blood draw. He retreated to the hallway and finished the conversation there.

"You were on the phone for a long time," Michele said once the tech returned to the lab and Jamison pocketed his phone. "You didn't make matters worse, did you?"

"Michele, please. Your mother can handle the truth."

Truth? She turned her gaze to the lime-green walls and the Norman Rockwell knockoff hanging over the stretcher.

Mildly annoyed with Jamison's reticence, Michele was more irritated at herself for causing the problem in the first place. With an ongoing investigation, the CID agent needed to be back at his office, and her mother needed to deal with the plans for the homecoming without having to worry about her daughter.

A nurse stuck her head through the door and smiled. "The lab needed to rerun a test. The results should be back shortly."

Shortly lapsed into thirty minutes of Michele trying to think of anything except Jamison standing guard in the hallway. Closing her eyes, she counted sheep but found the woolly animals even more stubborn than her CID bodyguard.

At some point, she must have dozed off. A noise from the hallway jerked her awake. Michele glanced up to find her mother standing in the doorway.

With three strides, Roberta closed the distance to where Michele lay and reached for her hand. "Jamison arranged for two nice military policemen to drive me here, and despite their assurances that you hadn't been hurt, I kept thinking of what could have been."

"I'm fine, Mother. As soon as the results come back from the laboratory, the doctor plans to release me."

"Which is what Jamison said." Roberta glanced back to where he stood in the hallway. "Why don't you come inside and wait with us, Jamison?"

Peering around her mother, Michele rolled her eyes to indicate how frustrated she was with Jamison's attempt to help. If he hadn't provided an escort to the hospital, her mother probably would have remained at home.

He ignored Michele's theatrics. "Thank you, Mrs. Logan. But I prefer the hallway."

Michele thought of another way to take him off guard duty. "Jamison arranged for my car and his to be brought to the hospital, Mother, so you can drive me home."

"Of course, dear." Roberta patted Michele's arm and then smiled at Jamison through the open doorway. "Don't let us hold you up, if you need to get back to post."

"It's not a problem, ma'am."

He returned her mother's smile, then grabbed the doorknob and fixed a steady gaze at Michele. "I'll be in the hallway until you're released from the E.R. Then I'm driving you home, Michele. Your mother can ride with us or drive back with one of the military policemen who brought her here. The other officer will follow us in your car."

With that, he closed the door, cutting off Michele's attempt to object. Irritated by his pronouncement of what would happen as well as the laboratory results that were taking much too long, Michele dropped her legs over the edge of the gurney, sat up and huffed.

"Jamison hasn't been in the best of moods since the ambulance brought me here."

"I'm sure he's just worried about you." Roberta patted Michele's arm. "I was worried, too, after you called. That's why I had to see for myself that you were okay."

"I'm fine, Mother." Even she was getting tired of the

pat response she offered whenever anyone questioned her well-being.

Roberta raised her hand to her neck and fiddled with the collar of her blouse. "And Lance's gravestone? Jamison said someone had vandalized the marker."

"One of the police officers mentioned a group of local teens who have been getting out of hand." Michele didn't bring up a possible connection between what had happened at the cemetery and the murder on post.

"The police wanted to know the last time anyone had visited the grave site," she said instead. "I said no one in the family had been there recently."

Her mother studied the picture on the wall of a young boy in a Boy Scout uniform, standing proud while his mother pinned a medal on his chest.

"Is that right, Mother?" Michele pressed.

Seemingly lost in her own thoughts, Roberta hesitated before she looked at Michele. "What did you say, dear?"

"How long has it been since you visited Lance's grave?"

"Not long." Roberta's response came too quickly. She bit down on her lip and turned toward the door just as it opened.

The doctor stepped into the room, a medical file in hand. "The lab results look good, Ms. Logan, and the X-rays were fine. Nothing broken. Remember, ibuprofen as needed, and take it easy for the next couple days. The muscle relaxers should help your back. Call if anything changes."

A nurse handed Michele her final paperwork and an aide pushed a wheelchair into the room as soon as the doctor had left. Once outside, Michele waited while Jamison retrieved his car.

"You have to be more careful, dear," her mother chattered at her side, her hand, once again, tugging nervously at her collar. "When I think what could have happened…"

"But it didn't. Besides, Jamison arrived immediately after the accident. He called the police and EMTs."

"And if he hadn't followed you to the cemetery, you could still be lying by the side of the road."

Although Michele knew her mother was right, she wouldn't waste time worrying about could-have-beens. Right now she wanted to go home and take a hot shower and change into something other than her rain-damp clothing.

Jamison pulled his sports car up to the curb. A military policeman parked behind him, and a second MP angled Michele's car into the lineup.

Roberta waved a greeting to the young man at the wheel of the second car before she turned back to Michele. "You ride with Jamison, and I'll go with the nice military policeman who brought me."

"Are you sure, Mother?"

Roberta nodded a bit too enthusiastically. "Of course, dear. Besides, you and Jamison probably have a lot to talk over."

Michele's mind was too fuzzy to override her mother. She had a headache and her left leg ached.

Jamison opened the passenger door and helped Michele out of the wheelchair. Wobbly as she was, she appreciated his strong arms supporting her. She inhaled the scent of him and, for an instant, rested her head against his shoulder, comforted by his closeness.

"Easy does it." His voice was filled with warmth as he gently ushered her forward.

Fighting off the desire to remain wrapped in his embrace, Michele slid onto the leather seat, feeling an instant weariness. She waited for Jamison to round the car and climb behind the wheel.

"I could have driven my own car back to post." Although she attempted to sound strong, the faint tremble in her voice spoke volumes about how she really felt.

"Not after that blow you took. You need to take it easy. The EMTs agreed, as I recall."

She nodded. "They did say something to that effect." The doctor had done so, as well, which she didn't mention. "I appreciate your help, Jamison, and hate tying up your day. I shouldn't have been so careless."

He put the car into gear and pulled onto the main road, heading back to Fort Rickman. "Stop blaming yourself for everything that happens, Michele. I never should have allowed you to drive to the cemetery alone. As soon as I realized your safety could be at risk, I raced to catch up to you." His eyes were filled with regret as he turned to look at her. "You weren't at fault, Michele. I was."

"I'm just glad you got there when you did."

He reached out and briefly squeezed her hand. "Have you remembered anything else about the driver?"

She shook her head. "Everything happened so quickly. All I could think about was getting out of the way."

"Thank God, you weren't seriously hurt."

The muscles in her neck tightened. "I'm not sure God had anything to do with it."

She turned toward the window. When they had dated, Michele's heart had softened to the message Jamison had shared about a loving God who wanted the best for His children. Jamison's enthusiasm and commitment to Christ had made her rethink what had happened to her brother and the reasons she had retreated from the Lord. She knew there was a higher power who gave life. Her problem was the seemingly fickle way in which He took that life away.

Oil and water didn't mix. Jamison was a believer and deserved someone who shared his faith. Not a woman who rejected anything to do with God.

"It's still about Lance, isn't it, Michele?"

Jamison deserved answers that she didn't know how to put into words. Michele worried her fingers and tried to pull the random thoughts pinging through her mind into some type of order.

"It's…it's not just Lance," she finally admitted. "Other things have happened."

"Like?"

What could she tell him? Like her father being wounded shortly after he had arrived in Afghanistan. Her mother had prayed for his safety, but God hadn't listened, just as He hadn't listened two years ago when Michele had asked God to keep Lance safe.

Fast-forward to when Michele's resolve had started to soften, and she had tentatively asked the Lord to watch over the CID agent she was beginning to care about in a very special way. Not long after that, her worst fears had been realized when the shooting on post almost claimed Jamison's life.

Suddenly chilled, Michele ran her hands over her arms.

"Cold?"

Without waiting for her reply, Jamison turned on the heat. She was grateful for his response to her unspoken need. Her body temperature had plummeted since she had gotten into the car.

"Why don't you close your eyes and relax?" Jamison suggested. Relieved she wouldn't have to answer any more questions, she settled back in the seat.

Her eyes grew heavy, probably from the muscle relaxer the doctor had given her. She drifted in and out of sleep, hearing snippets of a conversation Jamison had on his cell.

"She's okay, Dawson. We're headed back to post now. Tell Chief Wilson I'll brief him back at the office, once I ensure Mrs. Logan and Michele are safe at home."

Feeling the car decelerate, she blinked her eyes open, surprised they were already at her parents' quarters. Both military policemen parked behind Jamison. Roberta met them on the sidewalk, her cell phone in hand.

"Your father just called with good news. He pulled a few strings and got the general's approval to move up the brigade's return. If everything goes as planned, they should arrive Friday morning."

Michele attempted to smile. "That's wonderful news."

"Major Hughes will be on board the first plane." Roberta glanced at Jamison. "Stanley wants him escorted off the aircraft ahead of the other soldiers so he can be reunited with his children in a private area."

"I'll ensure that's taken care of, ma'am."

Supporting Michele's arm, he helped her from the car and guided her toward the house. "Security needs to be tightened for the homecoming ceremony, Mrs. Logan. It might be wise to schedule a briefing for the family members this evening. Although it's short notice, I can reserve the auditorium on post."

Roberta nodded. "The wives were already planning to get together tomorrow to make goody bags for the soldiers who don't have families. The barracks need to be swept out and dusted for the guys, the beds made, that type of thing. I planned to send a reminder email to the wives later this afternoon. Information about the briefing will be easy enough to add."

"I'd like to review some safety measures they can take around their homes, as well as the security we'll put in place at the airfield."

"Of course."

Michele and Jamison followed Roberta inside. A few of the wives had remained at the house and were still in the living room. They looked up as Michele excused herself to change clothes. She stopped on the stairway to hear her mother share the good news about the unit's return. The women seemed visibly relieved.

Michele felt just the opposite.

Bad news came in threes.

Yolanda had been murdered.

Lance's gravestone had been desecrated, and Michele had been wounded in a hit-and-run accident.

What worried her now was her father's safety during his last hours in Afghanistan.

Michele rubbed her hands over her arms to stave off the chilling anxiety that swelled up within her and filled her with dread. Until tomorrow morning when her father's plane took off, Michele would be waiting to learn if tragedy would strike again.

FIVE

Jamison stared after Michele as she climbed the stairs to the second floor of her parents' quarters, inhaling the scent of her perfume that still swirled around him. She had gone through so much today and seemed exhausted on the way home. Suggesting she rest in the car had provided the short-term reprieve she had needed.

Wanting to ensure that she was okay before he returned to CID headquarters, Jamison stepped into the kitchen and made a series of phone calls to reserve the post auditorium for the briefing that evening and line up the military police to patrol the area. His last call was to the Fort Rickman airfield to alert them about the returning flights on Friday and the need for secure arrangements for the reunion ceremony. The doorbell rang just as he disconnected.

Roberta greeted Chief Agent in Charge Wilson, a tall and muscular African-American who was the head of Fort Rickman's CID.

"Good to see you, Mrs. Logan, although I'm sorry about the circumstances." The chief pointed to Dawson who followed him into the foyer. "You know Special Agent Timmons."

"Yes, of course. We met earlier." She smiled as Jamison

joined them. "Agent Steele has been a great help both last night and today."

"Sir." Jamison nodded to his boss, then acknowledged Dawson. "Miss Logan just returned home from the hospital. Other than being tired and bruised, she seems okay."

Wilson turned to Mrs. Logan. "A relief to all of us, ma'am."

The few ladies who remained in the living room stood, gathered their purses and walked into the foyer, nodding to the CID agents on their way to the door. "Roberta, we need to be going."

Mrs. Logan escorted them outside to say goodbye. While she was gone, Jamison filled his boss and Dawson in on the brigade's new flight schedule. He also informed them of the wives' briefing that evening and the requests he had made for security from the military police.

The chief pursed his lips. "After what happened at the cemetery, I want round-the-clock protection for Mrs. Logan and her daughter."

Jamison was one step ahead of the chief. "I have two men stationed outside, sir, and two additional military police will be here shortly to provide increased surveillance."

"Excellent."

"The Freemont police are compiling names of people in town who may have visited the cemetery today," Jamison continued. "I want to question anyone who might have seen the black car that hit Miss Logan."

Wilson's eyes narrowed ever so slightly. "Agent Timmons can work with the Freemont police. You need to focus on Colonel Logan's family."

Jamison held out his hand. "Sir, I'm more than able to ensure their safety and handle the investigation."

"I'm not insinuating you can't, but Agent Timmons will be the lead investigator on this one. In addition to keeping the colonel's wife and daughter safe, I want you to coordinate security for the brigade's return."

Jamison swallowed his frustration. Although the shift was subtle, his relationship with the chief had changed after the shooting ten months ago, and not in a positive way. Being taken from the lead on this case drove home the point that Wilson wasn't pleased with his performance.

The front door opened, and Mrs. Logan stepped back inside. "Can I offer you gentlemen a cup of coffee?"

The chief shook his head. "Not for me, ma'am, but I would like to talk to you for a few minutes about Mrs. Hughes."

"Certainly." Mrs. Logan pointed to the living room. "We'll be more comfortable in here." Dawson and the chief quickly settled into two Queen Anne chairs across from the couch where she sat.

Unable to move forward, Jamison remained in the hallway, hearing his manipulative father's voice taunt him from the past. *"You'll always be a failure, Jamie-boy."*

Turning at the sound of footsteps, he watched Michele descend the stairs, bringing with her more of the sweet floral scent he had noticed earlier. Her hair was damp, and she had evidently showered before donning a flowing skirt and a silk top that hugged her slender body. She smiled, and the voice from his childhood disappeared.

"You look lovely," Jamison said, feeling a swell of emotion in his chest.

Before she could reply, the doorbell rang.

He glanced out the window. A beige van bearing the florist's shop logo was parked on the street. The florist stood on the steps, a bouquet of flowers in hand.

Surprise flickered from his eyes when Jamison opened the door. "Hey, sir. Long time no see. I've got a delivery."

"Miss Logan was in your shop earlier today, Mr. Sutherland. You could have saved yourself a trip."

Embarrassment tugged at his lips. "Actually, the order came in after she left. After you left, too, sir. And the flowers are for *Mrs.* Logan. Is she home?"

Gently nudging Jamison to the side, Michele reached for the bouquet. The arrangement included yellow roses and white mums with baby's breath and a few other varieties Jamison couldn't name. "They're beautiful. I'll give them to my mother."

Mrs. Logan excused herself from the living room. "Why, isn't that bouquet exquisite? Who are they from, dear?"

Michele opened the card. Her expression clouded ever so slightly as she read the card. "Dad sent them."

Mrs. Logan either didn't notice the change in Michele or refused to respond. Instead, she turned her gaze to the florist. "Thank you, Teddy."

"The pleasure is all mine, ma'am. Be sure to let me know when Colonel Logan plans to return to Fort Rickman so I can place the order for the welcome-home ceremony."

"If everything goes as scheduled, the unit should arrive on post Friday morning."

"I'll contact my wholesaler about the delivery." With a brief nod, he walked back to his truck. Jamison waited until the florist's van was out of sight before he closed the door.

Michele had taken the flowers into the kitchen. From where Jamison stood, he could see the colorful bouquet lying on the kitchen table. Sometimes he felt as if he were stumbling around in the dark without night vision goggles when it came to Michele. After she had run away to Atlanta, he had phoned her a number of times, but the calls always went to her voice mail. Finding out where she lived had been easy enough. The hard part had been trying to stay away from her.

One night when he had allowed his emotions to get the better of him, Jamison had driven to Atlanta and parked outside her apartment, trying to decide what to say when he knocked on her door. Just before he'd climbed from his car, Michele had stepped outside on someone else's arm.

Driving back to Fort Rickman that lonely night, he'd vowed to wipe her memory from his mind. The problem was he hadn't been able to remove Michele from his heart.

In hindsight, he should have sent flowers to woo her back or bouquets while they were dating to convince Michele that, despite the danger of his job, what they had was special.

No matter how he tried to rationalize her actions, he still felt betrayed. He had loved her once. Seeing Michele today, lying injured on the side of the road, had made him realize how much.

Michele leaned against the counter in the kitchen and stared at the flowers, feeling the lump that had instantly formed in her throat when she'd read her father's card.

Footsteps sounded behind her. She turned to find Jamison staring at her as if he could see the need written on her heart.

"What's wrong?" he asked, concern softening his gaze.

"Nothing." She wrapped her arms defiantly across her chest. "As I keep telling everyone, I'm fine."

Instantly she regretted the sharpness in her tone.

He bristled. Of course, he would.

If only he would join the other agents in the living room so she could have a moment to pull herself together.

He stepped toward her.

Needing a distraction, she grabbed scissors from a

drawer and reached for the bouquet. With quick decisive motions, she plucked a flower from the bunch and snipped off the lower end of the stem.

Jamison moved closer. "Was it something I said?"

"Of course not." Pulling in a deep breath, she tried to untangle the confusion she felt. "It…it was my mother."

Michele reached for a second flower. "She didn't mention why Dad sent the bouquet. He knew today would be hard on her."

"Because of Lance?"

Michele nodded. "She doesn't talk about my brother, although for some reason she did last night. I don't think she goes to the cemetery or leaves flowers at his grave. It's as if…"

Still aware of the medication's effect on her, Michele tried to gather her thoughts. "It's as if she doesn't want to deal with his death."

"Maybe that's her way of running away."

Michele glanced up at Jamison, knowing there was more to his statement than just her mother's response to losing a child. For a long moment, what was unspoken hung in the silence between them.

"We all handle grief in different ways," she finally said, reaching for a glass vase and another flower.

He watched her work and then wrinkled his face as if he had never seen anyone arrange flowers. "You cut off the ends of the stems?"

She ran water into the vase. "The blooms last longer when the old ends are trimmed away."

"Like a gardener prunes a bush or vine?"

She smiled. "You weren't a country boy, were you?"

"Hardly." He choked out a rueful laugh, brief and bitter. "More of a drifter. My dad and I moved often, usually in the middle of the night when he was running from the law."

Something he hadn't revealed to her when they were dating. "I take it your father wasn't the best of role models."

"That's an understatement." Jamison tapped his fingers on the counter as if to diffuse the nervous energy that came over him along with the memory of the past.

"Yet you're a good man."

He stopped tapping. She saw conflict in his eyes.

"So, who helped you growing up?" she asked, hoping to deflect the intensity of his gaze.

Jamison rolled his shoulders, perhaps to ease the tension she could see in his neck and splayed hands. "I threw the discus in high school. My coach encouraged me to go into the army. A chaplain when I was in basic training filled in more of the blanks. He taught me about working hard and doing my best."

Michele heard the admiration he had for both men in his voice and saw the stress lift ever so slightly from Jamison's physical bearing. The memory also brought a smile to his lips.

"The chaplain made his point to a bunch of green recruits by explaining how we needed to whittle away at the deadwood of the softer life we had lived before we came into the military. After a ten-mile road march, his message started to have meaning. By the time I graduated as the top trainee, I had taken his words to heart."

"Top trainee." Michele raised her brow. "That's impressive."

Jamison shoved off the praise with a shake of his head. "My drill sergeant takes all the credit, as well as the chaplain."

"Because he encouraged you to succeed?"

Jamison nodded, then paused for a moment as if thinking back to those beginning days in basic training. "In retrospect, he was probably talking about pruning, although he never used the word. He said changing was painful, but we would be stronger in the end."

Michele reached for another flower. Her fingers touched the fragile petals of the bloodred rose. "Losing someone I loved changed me—but it hasn't made me stronger."

He stepped closer. Too close. She could smell his aftershave, a masculine scent that reminded her of sea breezes. She couldn't help but think back to the nights she'd kissed Jamison on her doorstep and then come inside with the smell of him clinging to her hair. Those nights, she had fallen into bed, hugging her pillow and reliving his lips on hers.

As much as she wanted to change the subject, she couldn't. "Is Lance's death supposed to make me stronger?"

"Michele." He closed the gap between them.

She squared her shoulders, determined to remain in control. "What about Yolanda?"

"We live in the world, Michele. Evil exists. Bad people who do bad things exist, no matter how much we want to pretend they don't. We can't control what they do—only how we respond."

A roar filled her ears. She wrapped her arms across her chest and stepped back again, wanting to distance herself from Jamison and his hollow rhetoric.

Yolanda shouldn't have died, and Michele shouldn't have made a bad decision that resulted in her brother being on board the helicopter that fateful day. A decision everyone in her family refused to talk about.

As if in a dream, the memory from ten months ago of Jamison's blood-smeared white shirt returned unbidden. Dawson had been hit, but when she'd gotten the call about the shoot-out on post, Michele thought Jamison had been the one not expected to live.

She turned away, no longer able to look at Jamison, and fled into the hallway. Tears burned her eyes. Her hand grabbed the banister.

"Is something wrong, dear?" Her mother's voice came from the living room. "Michele?"

She didn't answer. She couldn't reply or she would break down on the stairway. At the landing, she turned into the first bedroom. Her room. Closing the door, she slipped the lock into place.

Lance's picture smiled at her from the dresser. She opened the top drawer and saw the Bible he had given her. A book she hadn't read since his death.

Her gaze fell on a small framed verse she'd received as a child. *All things work together for good to those who love God.*

After everything that had happened, she couldn't trust the Lord. Not now. Not ever.

A small wooden box nestled next to the Bible. Her fingers touched the wood, unwilling to open the lid. She pushed the drawer shut and fell onto her bed.

She clenched her eyes closed, hoping to block out the moment. Instead, her mind filled with the horrible vision of Yolanda's body.

"No." Michele shook her head and groaned.

Lance's funeral. The cloying smell of flowers surrounded his casket.

The minister's voice sounded in her ears. "The Lord giveth life and the Lord taketh away life."

Once again, she saw Jamison's blood-smeared white shirt, only this time he was dead.

"Why, Lord?" she cried. "Why do You always take the ones I love?"

SIX

Cell phone in one hand, Jamison gripped the steering wheel with the other as he talked to Dawson. "I'm on my way to the auditorium. Mrs. Logan and Michele should be along shortly in their own vehicle. Stiles will remain at the quarters while McGrunner follows the ladies. I told him to stick like glue to both of them."

"Mac's a good man."

"Who understands the importance of protecting the colonel's wife." Jamison's tightened his grip on the steering wheel. Just so long as Mac would keep Michele safe, as well.

"Were all the spouses notified about the briefing?" Dawson asked.

"Affirmative. Mrs. Logan sent out an email to the Family Readiness Groups earlier today. All the spouses should have received the information. Everyone has been waiting for word of the brigade's redeployment, so the briefing wasn't a total surprise, despite the short notice. Those who don't have internet access were contacted by phone."

"You checked the auditorium?"

"The building's clean. I've got men patrolling the parking lot and surrounding area. They'll remain on-site until everyone leaves the premises."

Dawson blew out a breath. "You're expecting the killer to show up tonight?"

"It's a possibility. Having that many people, mainly women, amassed in one area is a perfect opportunity for a psychopath to wreak havoc on Fort Rickman."

"Yet there's no indication he's on post."

"That doesn't mean he's not. I plan to stress that point when I brief the families tonight. I'll also discuss the welcome-home ceremony as well as the security issues at the airfield."

"I'll be glad when the brigade returns to post. Soldiers home from a war zone are a formidable protective force."

"Even then, we can't let down our guard until the killer is apprehended."

"We'll find him."

Jamison wasn't as confident. "What's happening with the press?"

"The commanding general is asking the media to go through the Public Affairs Office. They issued a statement, and so far everyone's been compliant."

"No one tied the run-in at the cemetery to the murder?"

"Not that I've heard so far. I contacted the Freemont police. They're still tracking down the names of townspeople who have relatives buried near the oak tree."

"Simpson was the officer at the cemetery today. He seemed competent."

"Freemont P.D. verified the blood on the gravestone was bovine, not human."

"Exactly as Simpson suspected." Jamison made a mental note to call the Freemont cop. "Did you discuss the autopsy with Major Hansen?"

"The doc seems to be as busy as we are. He finally returned my call. What he found was consistent with the victim's wounds. The autopsy revealed nothing we didn't already know."

"What about the Prime Maintenance man?"

"Danny Altman? Evidently he took a couple days' leave."

"Convenient." Jamison focused his gaze on the road ahead. "Any word from Special Agent Warner in Afghanistan?"

"Negative. You want me to call him?"

"I'll handle it."

"Listen, buddy—" Dawson hesitated. "I was as surprised as you were today when the chief gave me the lead on this case. You know I wouldn't go behind your back or ask for you to be taken off the investigation."

Jamison didn't want to rehash a decision the chief had already made. "Wilson's in charge. He did what he thought was right."

"It's not how it looks."

"He believes in you, Dawson. Let's leave it at that."

"But—"

"No buts. Just keep me informed," Jamison said before he disconnected.

Dawson was a good agent. A few months junior by date of rank to Jamison, but Dawson had excellent instincts and was a bulldog when it came to tracking down evidence. Plus, he could handle the pressure of both the chief and the commanding general demanding an arrest. As much as Jamison hated being removed from the investigation, finding the killer and putting him behind bars was the goal, no matter who took the lead.

Turning into the parking lot, Jamison flicked his gaze over the large freestanding auditorium. Military police stood guard at the doors, ready to check the identification cards of all who sought entry. Each MP had a list of spouses' names, which had been pulled from the master roster at the brigade. Anyone seeking entrance other than family members would be questioned. Purses and totes would be searched, and every precaution would be taken to ensure the safety of all those attending the briefing.

Leaving his car at the far side of the auditorium, Jamison double-timed toward the building. Once he confirmed that the proper security measures were being implemented, he stepped back outside and eyed the stream of cars heading into the parking lot.

Car doors slammed as women exited their vehicles and walked toward the large central structure. Despite the news of the unit's impending arrival, the women's eyes were solemn and their faces strained with worry—no doubt, because of Yolanda's death.

A light blue sedan turned into the lot. Michele sat behind the wheel, her mother next to her in the passenger seat. A military police cruiser followed close behind. As Michele parked, the cruiser pulled over to the curb where Jamison stood.

Corporal McGrunner, a tall Midwest farm boy with a lanky body and a ready smile, rolled down his window and saluted. "Both Mrs. Logan and her daughter are present and accounted for, sir."

"Anything happen at the Logan quarters after I left?"

Mac shook his head. "Negative. Except Mrs. Logan offered us sweet tea and chocolate chip cookies."

"I won't ask whether you succumbed to her Southern hospitability."

The MP's eyes twinkled. "Mrs. Logan can be insistent."

Jamison had to smile. "Remain outside, Mac. Keep watch. After the briefing, we'll escort the ladies back to their quarters."

"Yes, sir."

Jamison adjusted his tie as he hustled across the parking lot. He approached the sedan and held the door open for Mrs. Logan.

"Ma'am."

"Evening, Jamison."

Michele dropped the keys into her handbag. She stepped onto the asphalt and turned to close her door.

Their eyes met for an instant, causing a muscle in Jamison's jaw to twitch. "Evening, Michele."

"Jamison."

She wore a pretty dress that hugged her waist and flowed around her knees. A gentle breeze pulled at her hair. She arranged the wayward strains back into place and heaved a sigh that reminded him of her struggle earlier this afternoon.

"How's the leg?" he asked.

"Not as sore."

"And the muscle in your back?"

"Better."

A car turned into the lot and drove toward them. Jamison placed his hand on Michele's arm, warning her of the approaching vehicle.

Moved by her closeness, he tried to ignore the swell in his chest and guided her forward once the car passed. "Did you get some sleep?"

She nodded, her eyes on the pavement.

Evidently, she didn't want to talk.

He turned to Mrs. Logan. "Ma'am, as you probably know, the chaplain's been on temporary duty in South Carolina. He returned to post this afternoon and will be available if any of the women want to schedule an appointment. He also mentioned a prayer service tomorrow for the unit's safe return."

"You and the chaplain have thought of everything, Jamison."

"What are you planning to tell the ladies tonight?" Michele asked, raising her gaze.

Pointing Michele toward the auditorium, he tried to concentrate on what she had asked instead of her smooth skin and silky hair and the vulnerability he felt emanating from her whenever he got close.

"Basic safety with emphasis on being cautious. And I'll encourage those gathered to call us if they're concerned about anything. We've increased the number of phone lines coming into CID headquarters. Plus, we've set up a neighborhood watch program in each housing area. Luckily, some of the units aren't deployed, so we've got military personnel organized on foot patrols."

Michele raised her brow. "What about the women who live off post?"

"We haven't forgotten them," he said with a flicker of a smile. "The Freemont police have the names and addresses of all the military families in the surrounding area. They're organizing neighborhood watch programs, just as we are at Fort Rickman."

Mrs. Logan patted Jamison's arm. "I certainly appreciate all you're doing."

"It's my job, ma'am."

"Yes, but you go above and beyond." Her attention turned to a minivan that had just parked.

"Excuse me for a minute." Always the thoughtful colonel's wife, Mrs. Logan stepped toward the three wives who climbed from the van and greeted each of them with a warm embrace.

Jamison guided Michele across the street. His hand touched the small of her back, and her hair blew against his shoulder. For an instant, he had a sense of the world's being in right order.

Then he glanced at the military police standing at the entrance to the auditorium. With a killer on the loose, nothing was right tonight.

Tugging the free-flowing strains of her honey-brown hair behind her ear, Michele drew in a shallow breath. "I need to apologize about the way I acted earlier. The muscle relaxer made me tired and emotional."

He flicked his free hand, trying to dispel her concern. "Michele, it's okay. You've been through so much. No need to apologize for anything."

"I wasn't myself, Jamison. You know I'm usually levelheaded."

Levelheaded? Michele was beautiful in so many ways and stronger than even she realized, but while she tried to make good decisions—levelheaded decisions—she saw life through a prism that twisted reality.

"You've had two shocks in the last twenty-four hours that have taken a toll on you," he offered, knowing she was waiting for his response. "The hit-and-run accident today was stressful enough without what happened last night. Everyone reacts differently, and you need time to rest and heal. You probably should have stayed home this evening."

She shook her head. "I needed to be here for my mother. She seems in control on the outside, but she's struggling inside. Yolanda's death, compounded by the anniversary of Lance's crash. It's a lot to carry."

Michele was able to recognize her mother's struggle but not her own. The last rays of the setting sun shadowed her flushed cheeks and expressive brows raised in question as if she wanted him to agree.

When he didn't respond, she continued, her voice low

so only he could hear. "Even though Mother rarely talks about Lance, I know she's still grieving."

Michele was, as well. Jamison held his tongue, hoping she would make the transition to her own internal struggle. Exposing her pain would be healing, but as he waited for her response, he sensed she needed prodding.

"What about you, Michele? Are you still grieving?"

She stopped her forward progression and seemed to try to mask her own confusion by straightening her spine and raising her jaw. Although determination flashed from her eyes, he could read through her false bravado.

When they had dated, Michele had given him only a glimpse of what she held within. Now that they'd been thrown together again, he could see that her grief was still so raw.

Wanting to console her, he said, "You were lucky."

She titled her head and looked defiantly into his eyes. "In what way?"

"From what you've said, Lance was a great brother. You had a close relationship. The pain you feel is because you loved him. Some people don't grow up surrounded by love."

Jamison thought of his own childhood and his wayward father who didn't know anything about raising a child. "I can only imagine the blessings you experienced growing up. The affirmation alone—"

He had already said too much. She was starting to shut him out. Jamison had to stop, but he couldn't resist making one more attempt to pull down the wall she had built around her fragile heart.

"Some people—" He hesitated, needing to choose his words. "Some people don't know how to love. Treasure the close relationship you and your brother had, but don't allow it to keep you from living life in the present." Jamison struggled every day to keep his past from poisoning his happiness. He hated to see Michele suffering the same way.

In truth, his father had been a dysfunctional narcissist, who had taken everything from his young son and given him nothing in return. Nothing except condemnation.

"You're a failure, a good for nothin'."

Michele had grown up with strong role models who practiced loving, giving relationships. She would never be able to understand a man who thought the world owed him everything and who resented his son's drive and determination.

Only through the grace of God had Jamison been able to hold on to the truth. He didn't want a handout or a leg up, nor did he want to live on the dole like his old man. His refusal to compromise on that had destroyed any chance of a working relationship between him and his father, but it had allowed him to build new relationships that he treasured. Relationships with his colleagues. His friends. And God.

Jamison had worked hard to distance himself from his father and his past. The military had been a good influencer, and the chaplain who had taught him about the Lord had given him a firm foundation on which to stand.

But now the military community that had given him so much was in danger. That was why he had to push forward and right the wrongs and protect the innocent and catch the bad guys so no one else would get hurt. Jamison had to succeed. If not, he would turn into the person his father wanted him to be. A failure just like his old man.

Jamison caught up to Michele as she neared the security checkpoint at the entrance to the auditorium. Had they made any progress tonight? The fact was, he had revealed more than he needed to, which made him wonder about his own internal struggle. As usual, Michele had been more reticent.

She gave her name and handed her driver's license to the military policeman, who checked her off the roster. Jamison escorted her to a seat near the stage.

The woman next to her had rosy cheeks and expressive blue-green eyes and evidently knew Michele because they embraced in a long hug and talked about the last time they had been together.

"It must have been the battalion's homecoming," the rosy-cheeked woman said. "What was it, three years ago when the guys came back from Iraq?"

"Then you moved on to a new assignment. I didn't know Paul had been transferred back to post."

"He was reassigned to Fort Rickman five months ago," the woman explained. "Paul left for Afghanistan after we moved into quarters." Her smile waned. "I...I'm sorry about your brother. His death must have been hard on all of you."

Michele nodded and then glanced up at Jamison. "Have you met Special Agent Steele?"

"Alice Rossi." She extended her hand. "I'm Sergeant Paul Rossi's wife."

"Nice to meet you, ma'am."

Knowing Michele was in good company, Jamison excused himself and joined Mrs. Logan on the stage.

The seats in the auditorium quickly filled, and a buzz of conversation carried across the hall as the audience chatted among themselves.

Chaplain Grant, a tall lieutenant colonel with a long face and a sincere smile, joined them on the stage.

Jamison accepted his outstretched hand. "Thanks for being here, sir."

"Terrible what happened last night, Agent Steele."

"Yes, sir."

The chaplain stepped to where Mrs. Logan was sitting

in a folding chair. They talked about the prayer service scheduled the next day while Jamison scanned the crowd. His gaze came to rest on Michele, who continued to chat with Mrs. Rossi.

An unwelcome yearning filled Jamison that set him back to where he had been ten months ago. He had tried to convince himself that he had moved on with his life, but after being with Michele for these last twenty-four hours, he had to face facts. He still cared for the colonel's daughter.

At that moment, she turned and raised her eyes to meet his. Jamison's chest constricted. He needed to remember that everything had changed when Michele walked away from him.

No matter what he read in her gaze, Michele Logan didn't want anything to do with a military guy and especially a CID agent. Bottom line, she didn't want anything to do with Jamison.

Michele had trouble sitting through the briefing in the auditorium, mainly because Jamison was onstage. Seeing him dressed in his crisp white shirt and dark suit brought back memories of when they had dated.

Concern and compassion for the family members warmed his expression as he answered their questions and offered suggestions to keep everyone safe. He gave out his phone number, asking to be called if anyone had a problem or felt the least threat of danger.

"He certainly is a fine man," one of the wives said to a woman sitting behind Michele.

She had to agree. Jamison was a good man with a big heart and a willingness to help others. He believed in doing what was right and worked hard to keep military personnel and family members safe from anyone out to do them harm.

Michele had recognized his dedication and commitment when they had first met, although at that point in their relationship, she hadn't realized the danger he faced each and every day. The shoot-out ten months ago had brought that reality front and center and sent her running scared.

If Jamison worked in another profession, one that didn't require him to risk his life, she never would have left Fort Rickman.

After the few comments Jamison had made at her house today, she better understood his commitment to the military. His childhood had been difficult, and the army had provided stability and security and a feeling of being part of a team that was making a difference. It would be hard to let that go and move into the civilian world, no matter how much she wanted him to do exactly that.

On the stage, Jamison stood beside her mother, who continued to address the gathering. "The major portion of the unit is scheduled to leave Afghanistan tomorrow," Roberta said to those assembled. "If everything goes as planned, the planes should land at the airfield on post Friday morning. I'd ask you to please notify any of the spouses who aren't here tonight. Some of the families have been staying with relatives in other parts of the country and will be returning to Fort Rickman soon. We've activated the calling trees, and the rear detachment is trying to contact everyone not in the area, but you can help by spreading the word."

She glanced out at the audience and smiled. "Because this is such a difficult time, Chaplain Grant will be having a special prayer service at the Main Post Chapel tomorrow, at 11:00 a.m. We'll be asking the Lord to bring the brigade safely home and to protect us so we can all be reunited with our deployed loved ones."

Glancing down at her notes, she continued. "At 1:00 p.m. tomorrow, we'll meet at the brigade to get the barracks ready for the soldiers. We could use everyone's help. Also, we need baked goods and candy for the welcome-home goody bags each soldier will have waiting for him or her in the barracks." She smiled. "The work will keep us occupied while we await the brigade's return."

Motioning toward Jamison, she added, "Don't hesitate to call Special Agent Steele if you have any questions or concerns."

After a round of applause, the family members exited the auditorium. The night was hot and humid when Michele stepped outside. Her mother followed a few minutes later, surrounded by a group of women eager to discuss the brigade's new arrival date.

Alice Rossi had stopped to talk to some of the wives inside before she caught up with Michele. "It was good seeing you tonight."

"Don't you want to say hello to Mother?"

Alice glanced at the women gathered around Roberta. "She's busy, and I need to get home. Thank her for all she's done to help the wives while the brigade has been deployed. I'm sure she encouraged your dad to bring the unit back a few days early. After what happened to Mrs. Hughes, knowing the men will be home has been a big morale boost."

"Do you have to rush off?"

Alice's expressive eyes twinkled. "Paul said he'd call. It's our wedding anniversary, and I want to be home when he phones."

Michele smiled at the good news, which didn't seem to come often enough these days. "How many years?"

"Fifteen. Seems like only yesterday I was a new army wife. I wasn't sure where we'd go, but I wanted to be with Paul, no matter where the army sent him."

Michele thought of her own struggle. "Did…did you ever worry about his safety?"

Alice laughed. "Of course, but we made a pact early on in our marriage never to leave the house without a kiss and a prayer to keep us safe until we could be reunited. Trusting God helped me put aside any undue worry."

Michele held her tongue. Hadn't she prayed for her brother's safety?

"You'll be at the welcome-home ceremony?" Alice asked.

Michele nodded. "Yes, of course."

The wife squeezed her hand. "I'll see you there."

Watching Alice scurry to her car, Michele marveled at the lightness in her step, wishing she, too, could be free of the weight that seemed to always drag her down. No matter how much she longed to live in the moment and not worry about what tomorrow might bring, Michele couldn't change who she was and the way she reacted to fear.

Jamison was right. A lot had happened in a short amount of time. Hopefully, once her father was safe on U.S. soil, her outlook would improve.

Glancing over her shoulder, she peered into the auditorium where Jamison stood, still surrounded by women. Even from this distance, she could see how focused he was on those who needed more information or had questions. His broad shoulders seemed strong enough to bear the concerns and fears of all the wives.

Michele trusted Jamison, but she couldn't trust her heart to a man who placed himself in danger.

One of the wives hurried from the auditorium and edged close to Michele. She held a tote bag in her left hand. "I found this on the floor where Alice Rossi was sitting. She was in a hurry to get home and must have left it behind."

Michele pointed to the car disappearing in the distance. "Alice just drove away."

The woman rummaged in the bag. "Her cell phone's here, so we can't call her. I've got to pick up my kids at the babysitter's or I'd drop it off at her house."

Overhearing the conversation, Roberta excused herself from the group of ladies and reached for the bag. "You need to get your children. Michele and I can take the tote to Alice." Relieved, the woman hugged Roberta before she raced to her car.

Michele glanced back at Jamison still answering questions in the auditorium. Her mother followed her gaze.

"Looks like he'll be tied up for quite a while." Roberta pointed to Corporal McGrunner, standing nearby on the curb. "I'll see if Mac can escort us home."

"Jamison wanted to follow us, Mother."

"I know, dear, but you said Alice is expecting Paul to call. If so, she'll need her cell phone."

"I had the feeling he was calling on their home landline."

"Either way, she'll want her bag. I'll talk to Jamison and Mac while you get the car."

By the time Michele pulled up to the curb, Mac had climbed into the military police sedan. Roberta opened the passenger door and slipped into the seat next to her daughter.

"I sent one of the wives back inside to tell Jamison. Mac's in his car and ready to follow us."

Michele raised her brow. "Are you sure what we're doing is okay with Jamison?"

"Yes, dear."

Roberta gave Michele directions to Alice's house, but

she continued to worry. Pulling out her cell, she hit Speed Dial. "I'm phoning Jamison."

The call went to voice mail. Michele left a message, explaining why she and her mother hadn't waited for him.

As they left the parking lot, Michele glanced in her rearview mirror at the stream of cars behind them. "Mac appears to be caught in a traffic jam."

Roberta glanced over her shoulder at the bottleneck. "We should go ahead. I want to get home as soon as possible. I'm sure Mac will be along shortly."

"I'd feel better if we wait."

"You know how hard it is for the guys to place a call from Afghanistan. I don't want Alice to come back to the auditorium for her tote and miss the call." Roberta nudged her daughter. "Go on. Drive. I've got Jamison's cell number programmed on my phone. I'll call him if we run into a problem."

Roberta's voice sounded tired. The day had been long for both of them. There was no reason for Michele to make more of the situation than was needed. The detour to Alice's house wouldn't take long, and they would probably arrive at her parents' quarters before Jamison realized they had left the area.

Roberta pointed to the upcoming intersection. "Turn left at the light. Alice lives in the Harding Housing area at the southern edge of post."

Once the housing area came into view, Michele noticed headlights in her rearview mirror and smiled. "Looks like Mac caught up with us."

Roberta glanced back. "That's good, dear."

Michele felt a sense of relief. Although she had complied with her mother's wishes, she hadn't been able to shake the sense they were making a mistake.

Jamison had been so insistent about their need for protection. Usually, he was overly cautious. This time she agreed with him, yet the briefing had gone well, and none of the wives had mentioned any concerns at their own homes. Many of the women sitting around her had talked about Yolanda's death being a random killing, which had probably been the case.

Michele was tired and her leg ached. Just like her mother, she wanted to get home. Turning into the housing area, she glanced again at the vehicle following behind them. Her optimism plummeted when the car continued straight ahead on the main road.

Roberta pointed to the next intersection. "Turn right. Alice lives at the end of that road."

Michele reached for her cell. "I'm calling Jamison again. Something happened to Mac. Did you explain we were making a stop before heading home?"

Roberta tilted her head and hesitated. "He said he'd follow us."

Michele hit Speed Dial and sighed when she was, once again, connected to voice mail.

"Mother and I are making a quick stop in the Harding Housing area," she said into the phone. "Mac got tied up leaving the auditorium parking lot. We'll be delayed arriving home. Don't worry, we're fine." Breathing a bit more easily, she returned her cell to her pocket.

"Jamison is probably still talking to the ladies," Roberta said. "We'll be pulling into our driveway before he ever gets your message."

"Maybe so, but I don't want him to worry."

Roberta raised her brow. "I didn't know you were so concerned about Jamison."

"He's in charge of our security, Mother. I've caused him enough problems already."

"I don't think you're a problem, dear."

Before Michele could question the meaning behind her mother's last comment, Alice's house appeared at the end of the street. Pulling the sedan over to the curb, Michele glanced at the small quarters. The lights were on inside, although the blinds were drawn and the front stoop was dark.

Michele grabbed the tote and stepped onto the pavement. "Stay in the car, Mother. I'll be right back."

Roberta's cell phone rang. "Maybe that's Jamison."

She read the name on the screen. "It's Erica Grayson." She waved to Michele. "Go on, dear, while I find out if Yolanda's sister arrived."

Michele slammed the car door and hurried along the sidewalk to the house. As she neared the porch, she heard a telephone ring inside the quarters. Paul was calling on their landline.

Knocking lightly, Michele eased the front door open. "Alice? You forgot your tote bag at the auditorium. I'll leave it in the dining room."

Stepping inside, Michele placed the bag on the table. The phone rang again.

"Alice?"

Why didn't she answer the expected call?

A hallway led into the darkened kitchen. The phone rang a third time.

Michele's heart pounded a warning.

A shuffling noise sounded behind her.

She turned.

A man, wearing a black face mask, lunged from the shadows. He held a stun gun in his hand, aimed at her arm.

Ice-cold panic froze her for half a heartbeat before he released the charge.

Fire exploded through her body.

Her muscles convulsed and her limbs writhed in spastic movements she couldn't control.

His maniacal laughter filled the house and sent even more involuntary tremors to twist her spine.

She fell to the floor, tried to scream and heard only the deep guttural groan that came from her drooling mouth.

He grabbed her shoulder and flipped her over. The black ski mask leaned into her line of vision.

Michele tried to backpedal along the floor, but her legs wouldn't respond.

A knife. Razor sharp.

She gasped.

Unable to move, Michele could only think of Jamison, who tried so hard to protect her.

This time, he would be too late.

SEVEN

After the last woman thanked him for his help, Jamison hurried from the auditorium and searched the near-empty parking lot, frowning when he was unable to find Michele or her mother.

Anxiety threaded through his veins and headed straight for his heart. Surely he was overreacting. Corporal Mc-Grunner had probably escorted the women home.

Jamison pulled out his cell phone. Three voice mails. The first was from Michele. "We have to stop by Alice Rossi's house on the way home. Mac's following us, so you needn't worry."

Jamison couldn't calm the alarm clanging through his head. He tapped into the second message. Corporal Mc-Grunner's voice. All Jamison could hear was the worry in the soldier's usually calm baritone.

"Sir, I was following Mrs. Logan and her daughter back to their quarters. A traffic jam formed as I was getting out of the parking area and onto the main road. I…ah… Well, sir, they drove on. As soon as I could get free, I headed along the route we used earlier, but I can't locate them. I'm at their quarters now, and Stiles is the only one here. What should I do, sir? Where should I look?"

Jamison's gut tightened. Shoving aside his need to

punch a hole in the brick wall of the auditorium, he raced to his car and hit the prompt for the third call.

Michele's voice. Maybe everything was all right after all. When he listened to the voice mail he felt anything but relieved.

"Mac got tied up leaving the auditorium parking lot. We'll be delayed arriving home. Don't worry, we're fine."

Don't worry! As if he could do anything but worry. The two women had gone off alone. Exactly what Jamison had told them not to do. Slipping behind the wheel, he dialed Michele. Before the call went through, his phone buzzed.

Mrs. Logan's name appeared on the screen. Mother and daughter were probably back at their quarters, but Jamison couldn't hide his frustration as he raised the phone to his ear. "Where are you, ma'am? Corporal McGrunner lost you. Tell me you're all right."

"Oh, Jamison…something's happened…Michele…"

A sickening feeling swept over him, making his head swim and his ears ring. He backed out of the parking space and stomped on the accelerator, leaving a black line on the roadway.

"Where are you, ma'am?"

"Alice Rossi's place in the Harding Housing area. Quarters Thirty-seven."

"Is Michele with you?"

"That's the problem. She went inside to return Alice's tote bag. She…" Mrs. Logan gasped. "She never came out. I pounded on the door and tried to get in, but—"

"Michele's inside?"

"I saw a man through the sidelight window. He ran from the room when he heard me knock but he's still in the house." Roberta's voice broke.

"Get back in your car. Lock the doors and drive to the

military police headquarters. I'll have McGrunner meet you there."

Once again, Jamison had failed to keep Michele safe.

Disconnecting from the colonel's wife before she could respond, he hit Speed Dial for Dawson and relayed the address Mrs. Logan had given him. "We need every military police officer in that area. The perpetrator is holed up inside with Michele. Use caution approaching the house. Have Otis contact McGrunner. Mrs. Logan's on her way to the military police headquarters. Have Mac meet her there."

"Roger that."

Jamison shoved his cell phone into his pocket and gripped the steering wheel with both hands. He increased his speed and drove like a madman toward the housing area.

Please, Lord, keep her safe. Just because I couldn't protect her doesn't mean You won't.

If anything happened to Michele, Jamison would never stop blaming himself. For the first time, he began to understand Michele's hesitancy to embrace the Lord. In her mind, God hadn't saved her brother, so she refused to turn to Him in her need. The difference was that Jamison knew if he didn't put his trust in the Lord, everything he believed in would be a lie.

The drive across post took too long. Jamison's heart threatened to explode as he screeched to the curb, jumped from his car and raced toward the Logans' vehicle still parked on the street. Mrs. Logan sat huddled in the passenger seat.

"Get out of here." He waved her on. "Now. Corporal McGrunner is on his way to MP headquarters. You'll be safe with him. I'll take care of Michele."

She cracked the window, her eyes filled with fear, and

pointed to the thicket behind the quarters. "I...I just saw a man run into the woods."

Jamison flicked his gaze into the tall stand of trees.

"Drive away, ma'am."

She shook her head. Tears welled up in her eyes. "Michele has the keys. Besides, I...I won't leave my daughter."

"Then get down and stay put."

She slumped lower in the seat. Her muffled sobs cut through Jamison's resolve.

He darted up the front steps and crouched at the side of the door. Glancing through the sidelight, he saw nothing, heard nothing except his own heart thumping in his chest.

The fingers of his right hand tightened on his weapon. He reached for the brass knob with his left and groaned silently when it failed to turn.

Needing to get inside as soon as possible, he took a running leap and lunged, throwing his body against the door. Once. Twice.

The lock sprang, and the door flew open.

Weapon raised and finger on the trigger, he entered the house, his eyes searching the darkness.

A moan brought bile to his gut. He followed the sound into the dining room and dropped to the floor when he saw Michele.

Blood spattered the front of her blouse.

He touched her neck.

She blinked her eyes open. "Al...Alice?"

"What happened?"

"My muscles...spasms...I tried to fight, but...I couldn't move...."

"Did you see him?"

She nodded. "He...he was wearing a black ski mask.... He had a knife."

Jamison pushed back her hair, searching for the source

of the blood, relieved to find none. At the same time he raised his cell and called Dawson.

"Send an ambulance. I've got Michele. The guy ran. Set up roadblocks. Have foot patrols search the housing area. Lock down Fort Rickman."

"Alice?" she asked again when he disconnected.

"I'll find her."

Michele tried to sit up. Jamison put his hand on her shoulder. "Stay where you are."

He headed for the kitchen and adjoining breakfast area. The woman Michele had introduced him to at the auditorium lay on the floor beside the table. Her blue-green eyes had been full of life earlier. Now they were covered with a deadly haze.

He stooped and felt for a pulse. Faint, but she was still alive. "Hang on, ma'am. An ambulance is on the way."

Her neck had been cut, but the artery was still intact. She was lucky, or would be if she lived.

He heard a noise and turned.

Michele was standing in the doorway. She gasped and ran to kneel beside the wounded woman. "Oh, Alice."

Jamison checked the rest of the house. Glass from a small window next to the back door had shattered onto the floor. Easy enough for the perpetrator to stick his hand through the window and turn the lock, which must have been the mode of entry.

Jamison retraced his steps to the kitchen. He found Michele holding Alice's hand and reassuring her with a calming voice. "Hold on, honey. You're going to be okay."

Glancing up, Michele shook her head.

"The ambulance is on the way," he offered for support.

"Will it get here in time?"

Before he could respond, the house phone rang.

They both stared at where it sat on the kitchen counter.

"It's her wedding anniversary." Michele's voice was no more than a whisper. "Her husband said he'd call."

If Sergeant Rossi was on the line, Jamison would have to tell him about his wife. He glanced once again at Michele, her lips tight, her eyes wide.

Pulling his handkerchief from his pocket, Jamison wrapped it around the receiver and raised the phone to his ear.

"I used a stun gun." A muffled male voice. No hint of a Southern drawl.

Jamison needed to keep him talking. "How'd you get inside the house?"

"You're smart enough to figure that out."

"You attacked Yolanda and now Mrs. Rossi. Why?"

"I thought you were good at what you do."

"You've got a grudge against the military."

Laughter.

Jamison's fisted his free hand, wanting to reach through the phone and yank the killer by the throat.

The laughter halted abruptly. "I love the military, but not everyone acts heroically."

"Is killing an innocent woman heroic?"

A growl sounded in Jamison's ear. "I defended my country. I went to war and came home, but—"

"But what?"

"It was too late."

"Too late for what? Were you hurt?"

"I died." The line disconnected.

"Wait—" Jamison tapped in the digits to retrieve the caller's number.

Using his own cell, he phoned CID headquarters. Corporal Raynard Otis answered.

"The killer called the Rossi quarters." He relayed the

home phone digits and the incoming number. "See if you can find where the call originated."

"I'm on it, sir."

"What'd the killer say?" Michele asked when Jamison hung up.

"That he was a soldier who was redeployed home from the war too late."

Sirens wailed toward the house. Jamison started toward the front door, but stopped when the phone rang again. Just as before, he used his handkerchief and raised the phone to his ear, expecting to hear the killer's voice once more.

"Happy anniversary to the most beautiful woman in the whole world. I'm coming home, baby. Won't be long and you'll be in my arms."

Jamison's mouth went dry.

"Alice?"

"Sergeant Rossi, this is CID Special Agent Jamison Steele. I have bad news."

Michele clutched Alice's hand and watched Jamison's face as he explained what had happened to her husband over the phone. All too vividly, Michele remembered the call from her parents when Lance's chopper crashed.

The scream of sirens stopped out front, and the house filled with military police. EMTs hastened to help Alice. Michele moved away to give them room to work.

Jamison hung up with Sergeant Rossi as Dawson walked toward him. The two men lowered their voices. Jamison was a few inches taller than Dawson and leaner. His neck was taut, his gaze intense as they conversed.

They turned in unison and looked at Michele. Still overcome with fatigue, she stared back, unable to mask her fear. Another woman had been injured—almost killed—and the attacker had come after her.

Dawson approached her. "Jamison told me you saw the attacker."

"Yes, but I can't tell you what he looked like. He wore a ski mask and surgical gloves on his hands, like a doctor. His eyes were dark. Maybe brown, but I'm not sure."

"Any other features you recall? Height? Build?"

"Everything was a blur."

"Take your time," Dawson said.

She glanced from the lead agent to Jamison. His jaw was set and his eyes were dark. Ten months ago, Jamison's eyes sparkled, and his easy smile used to make her insides quiver. Right now the raw look on his face had her quivering again. Both of them knew she was lucky to be alive.

Michele and her mother never should have left the auditorium without Jamison. But then another thought struck Michele full force. If Jamison had escorted them, he would have confronted the killer. Knowing what could have happened to Jamison mixed with the memory of the knife and the spasms that had rocked her body.

"He was medium height," she finally said. "Well built. Like Jamison."

"Caucasian?" Dawson asked.

"Yes." She thought again of the knife and saw his hands holding the sharp blade. This time, she saw the knife at Jamison's throat.

Jamison stepped closer."Is there anything you can tell us about the knife, Michele?"

She closed her eyes and rubbed her hands over her forehead, forcing her mind to focus on Jamison's question instead of the image of the sharp blade and Jamison's exposed flesh.

"Metal handle?" he asked.

She nodded.

"Serrated blade or smooth?"

"Smooth. Sharp." She pursed her lips and shook her head. "The killer put it against my—" She touched her neck. "He stopped when someone pounded on the door."

Jamison nodded. "Your mother was worried about you. When she couldn't get in the house, she called me."

He leaned close to Michele as if he were trying to support her with his presence. She wished the others would go away so she could step into his arms. At the moment, with her insides still shaky and the memory of what had happened all too real, she wanted to be surrounded by his strength.

Looking into his eyes, a flash of connection passed between them, and she knew in that instant that Jamison understood.

"The effects of the stun gun will pass, Michele," he said, his voice soothing her fears. "The fatigue is due to your muscles convulsing and the lactic acid buildup."

"I…I'm the lucky one." She turned her gaze to the EMTs. They lifted Alice onto a gurney, ready to take her to the ambulance.

A medic approached Michele. "Ma'am, I'd like to check your vitals and see how you're doing."

"I…I'm okay."

"Yes, ma'am. But it's a good idea to let us make sure your stats coincide with how you feel."

Jamison's hand rubbed against her arm. "Dawson and I will be outside."

"My mother?"

"An MP is with her," Dawson said. "I'll tell him she can come in now."

Michele nodded. She didn't want Jamison to leave her. As she watched him walk away, she felt empty, drained, unable to think of anything except the urge to call him back to her.

Had she made a mistake by leaving him ten months ago? As much as she wished everything was different, she knew there was no way she could change what had happened. She had left Jamison for a good reason, or so it had seemed at the time. Now she wasn't sure of anything.

Once the signal was given, the military policeman allowed Mrs. Logan into the house. "Michele's in the kitchen," Jamison said as she rushed past him.

The two agents stepped outside. "How'd Michele end up with the killer?" Dawson asked.

Jamison explained about the tote bag and Michele and her mother trying to be Good Samaritans.

"Was he waiting for Mrs. Rossi to return home from the briefing? Or was he going through the house for some other reason, and she surprised him?"

"Nothing was disturbed, Dawson. He was there for one reason and one reason only. He targeted Yolanda Hughes and Alice Rossi. We need to find a tie between those two women. From what Michele said, he would have killed her if Mrs. Logan hadn't pounded on the front door and scared him off."

Jamison thought of the cemetery. Surely it was too much of a stretch to think the killer on post was the same person as the hit-and-run driver. Another thought chilled him. Could two attackers be targeting the same group of women?

Dawson's cell rang. He raised it to his ear and nodded. "Keep searching." When he disconnected, he turned worried eyes to Jamison. "We set up roadblocks as soon as you called. Teams are canvassing the surrounding area on foot. No sign yet of anyone suspect."

Jamison pointed to the area behind the house. "The

woods lead to the vast training area. If he headed that direction, he could be anywhere."

Dawson's gaze narrowed. "Plus, he could exit the post from one of the back roads. If what he said to you on the phone is true, he's prior military. Anyone previously stationed at Fort Rickman would know the post as well as the outlining ranges and training areas."

"He loves the military, but claims he died when he came home."

"Maybe he was injured," Dawson suggested.

"Or watched a comrade die."

"Or something happened when he came home."

"A wife left him perhaps? A family member died?" Jamison stared into the night. All around him, the crime scene team scurried to capture evidence.

"The husbands of the two victims currently serve in Colonel Logan's brigade, but they don't work together." Dawson mentioned what they both knew.

Jamison rubbed at his jaw. "But they served together under Logan when he took his battalion to Iraq. The unit came home three years ago. If that's the common thread, what would trigger the killer to strike now?"

"A relative in the battalion could have died in combat. If the killer identified with the deceased, he might start to believe he himself had served."

Jamison slapped Dawson on the back. "Which is why we need that list of names from the cemetery in Freemont. I'll give Simpson another call."

Pulling out his phone, Jamison tapped in the digits for the Freemont P.D. Simpson wasn't on duty. Neither was the other police officer, Bobby Jones, who had accompanied Simpson to the cemetery.

A third cop claimed Simpson had made some progress in tracking down the family members and would return

Jamison's call in the morning. He hung up less than satisfied and turned back to Dawson.

"You better contact the cemetery director first thing tomorrow. See if he can provide the information we need. Also, find out if anyone in the brigade has been killed during this deployment. A grieving father, a brother, even the son of a deceased soldier might want to cause problems for Colonel Logan when he brings his unit back this time."

Dawson nodded. "I'll check it out."

"Keep exerting pressure. We need a breakthrough on this case."

Again Dawson shrugged and flicked an embarrassed gaze at Jamison. "I told you, buddy. I didn't ask to take over the lead."

Jamison held up his hand. "Let's just get it done."

The blond agent shook his head. "Yeah, but the killer has struck twice. Add what happened at the cemetery and we've got three incidents. As far as finding the killer goes, we're batting zero."

Jamison stared into the darkness. His stomach roiled as he thought of what the killer had planned to do. The two of them were on opposite sides. The perpetrator wanted Michele dead. Jamison, if he did nothing else, had to ensure that Michele stayed alive.

Ten months ago, she had made it perfectly clear she didn't want Jamison in her life, but he would sacrifice everything to ensure that she had a life to live.

Even if it meant she'd leave him once again.

EIGHT

Michele huddled in the passenger's seat next to Jamison. Her mother sat directly behind her in the rear, lost in her own thoughts.

The three of them had followed the ambulance to the Fort Rickman Hospital and remained in the waiting room as Alice had been rushed into surgery. She'd come through that ordeal and was now in intensive care, monitored by a roomful of machines and a bevy of nurses and doctors who had insisted they go home. The medical staff promised to call at any change in her condition. Whether Alice would be strong enough to pull through was the question.

Physically drained, Michele knew her mother and Jamison had to be equally fatigued. On the ride home, they all seemed lost in their own worlds. Michele kept thinking about Alice and her husband and the prayer they must have said for his safety when he left for Afghanistan. It was doubtful either of them thought Alice would be the one critically injured and fighting for her life.

Overcome with the irony, Michele sighed.

Jamison turned to gaze at her, his face bathed in the half-light from the dash. Although her heart was heavy, she appreciated the concern she saw in his bittersweet smile.

"I'm glad the E.R. doc checked you out." He reached over the consol to take her hand.

She appreciated the warmth of his touch. "Two hospital visits in one day isn't a habit I want to continue."

He nodded. "I agree."

Turning her gaze toward the window, she thought of the killer still on the loose. What kind of man would attack so vengefully? Yolanda and Alice were wonderful women. Why had they been victims of such heinous attacks?

As much as she wanted to forget what had happened, the memory of the killer kept circling through her mind. She had looked into his eyes and had seen evil. Jamison had talked about bad people in the world. She was beginning to think he had sugarcoated the reality of whom they were up against.

Always considerate of her needs, Jamison helped her from the car when they arrived at her parents' home. The effects of the stun gun had been short-lived, but Michele gladly accepted his steadying arm and the attention he showered over her.

Once inside their quarters, Roberta made a pot of coffee, which she served to Jamison and Michele at the dining room table. Despite the mug she held, Michele still felt cold and longed, once again, for Jamison's hand to cover hers with warmth.

She stared at him from across the table. He had a string of questions for her mother, and from the intensity of his gaze, Michele realized he had slipped back into military CID mode.

"Can you recall anyone in the past that might have had a grudge against your husband, Mrs. Logan?"

She shook her head slowly. "No one who made his or her grievances known. I'm sure some of the soldiers were disgruntled from time to time if Stanley canceled their leave or kept their battalion in the field for an extended period of time. But if you're talking about anything significant, then I'd have to say no."

Michele wondered if he was getting too far off track. "Do you really think a person would attack women on post to get back at my father?"

Jamison sighed as if he, too, regretted the need to probe into brigade affairs. "We have to consider any situation that would make someone strike out, Michele."

Well aware that he was the expert in such matters, Michele held back from saying anything else and sipped her coffee.

Turning back to Roberta, Jamison continued, "Did any soldiers lose their lives under your husband's command?"

"A sergeant in his battalion died in Iraq. Stanley flew home with the body. Both of us attended the funeral."

"He was from the local area?"

Roberta nodded. "He had graduated from Freemont High School and had been the captain of the football team. Everyone loved him. His mom had died of cancer two years earlier, and he was an only child. It broke my heart to see his father grieving. I'll never forget him standing at the cemetery by the grave site."

"The Freemont Cemetery where your son is buried?"

Roberta nodded. "That's right."

"Do you recall the soldier's name?"

"How could I forget? Sergeant Brandon Carmichael. His father was so proud of him."

"What about this current rotation, ma'am?"

"The Lord's been good to us, Jamison. No loss of life."

Michele placed her mug on the table and rubbed her fingers over her arms. "Don't be too hasty, Mother. The brigade hasn't left Afghanistan yet."

Roberta patted Michele's hand. "Your dad's going to make it home."

Michele stood and stepped away from the table. "You were equally sure Lance would be okay."

Her mother's expression clouded. "You've got to stop blaming yourself."

"I'm not blaming anyone except the army."

"Accidents happen, Michele." Although Jamison's eyes were filled with concern, his voice was matter-of-fact, as if death was an acceptable part of military life.

She bristled and turned to gaze out the window into the night.

Her mother stepped toward her. "You still feel responsible for what happened to Lance."

"Do I?" She quirked her head at the woman she loved but didn't always understand. "How would you know, Mother? We never talk about him."

Roberta held out her hands. "What can I say that would change your mind?"

"You can tell me I made a mistake. Lance wouldn't have been in the helicopter if I had visited him."

"But you made the right decision, dear."

The phone rang. Roberta hesitated as if questioning whether she should answer. Checking the caller ID, she turned apologetic eyes toward her daughter. "It's Erica Grayson. She probably has information about Yolanda's funeral. I should take the call."

"Of course," Michele said, her energy drained.

Roberta stepped into the living area, phone in hand.

Michele grabbed her mug and headed for the kitchen, hoping a second cup of coffee would help clear her head.

Jamison followed. "You want to talk?"

"You don't need to get involved with our family problems."

"Whatever you need is what I want, Michele."

She would have laughed except she knew why she had left him and how much she had missed him over the last ten months. "I'll pretend I didn't hear that last statement."

He stepped closer, seemingly oblivious of the real root of the problem between them. "You may not want my input, but your mother's right. You haven't worked through your brother's death."

Anger rose within her. She pointed a finger back at herself. "It's not my problem, Jamison. It's my mother's problem and your problem. I keep telling everyone I'm fine, but no one believes me."

The sound of her mother's voice came from the living room. Roberta Logan—a woman who would have done anything for her daughter—was talking on the phone to one of the brigade wives who needed support. Michele had needed her mother's support when her brother died, but Roberta had gone back to helping with all the wives' activities and hadn't been able to reach out to her only remaining child.

Michele didn't want to talk about what had happened, yet the words spilled from her mouth as if they had a will of their own. "Remember when that last big storm hit the coast of Georgia?"

Jamison nodded. "Wasn't it about two years ago?"

"That's right. Homes were destroyed. People needed food and water. My insurance company wanted to provide hands-on help as well as aid with the insurance claims. We filled a number of trucks with nonperishable items, water, blankets."

Jamison's open gaze encouraged her to go on.

"Days before the storm, Lance had invited me to visit him for a long weekend. I planned to drive to Fort Knox, his new duty station. Then my boss asked for volunteers to help with the coastal relief, so I canceled my plans to be with Lance."

Truth was, she had chosen to help the storm victims because she was beginning to buy into the gospel message about helping others, which Lance always said was the Christian thing to do.

"If I hadn't chosen to help those people, Lance would have been on leave instead of in the helicopter that terrible day."

Jamison reached for her. "You're not to blame."

She jerked away from his touch. "How would you know? You put yourself in danger after my father left for Afghanistan. You knew I was worried because of the Afghani strikes we kept hearing about on the news and the attack he had already been involved in, yet you walked into that ambush on post. Did you think by praying to God you could put yourself in the line of fire and not suffer the consequences?"

His face clouded. "Oh, Michele, I…"

"You what, Jamison? You weren't thinking about the danger, were you? You probably had your Bible in one hand and your gun in the other and thought nothing could harm you."

He shook his head. "I made a mistake."

"A mistake? Do you know what that did to me when I heard about the shoot-out? I raced to the hospital and saw the stretcher being wheeled into the E.R. I learned later that Dawson had taken the hit, but at the time, I thought you were the one not expected to live."

"I'm sorry, Michele."

"Sorry isn't what I want for my life. I thought we were good together and wanted something long-term. I saw us growing old with kids and grandkids." She laughed ruefully, but tears stung her eyes. "The day of the ambush brought home the truth I'd been ignoring. With you, my future would be at a cemetery with the honor guard folding your flag and the commander presenting it to me with the thanks of a grateful nation."

She pointed into the dining room where Lance's flag sat on the buffet. "That's all we have left of my brother's memory. He doesn't have the luxury of falling in love and marrying a nice girl who will bear his children. All we have is a flag."

Jamison reached for her, but she shook her head. She didn't want his touch. She wanted him to admit he could see the truth.

"A flag doesn't bring comfort or grandchildren for my parents. Lance was a believer, Jamison. And so are you, but you can't count on God. The only one you can count on is yourself."

"Oh, Michele, you've got it all wrong."

She shook her head, not wanting to hear anything he had to say. "God doesn't want good things for His children. He wields His might with a fickle hand. Maybe He likes to see His children in pain so they turn to Him. That's what I would have if we were together. Pain and grief and a flag to remember what could have been. That's not enough."

She had to leave. She couldn't stand the look of disbelief on his face or the pity in his eyes. She wanted his love but without the military, without the constant danger and the chance she could lose him when she least expected. She had received one phone call that had broken her heart when Lance's helicopter crashed. A second phone call had informed her of the shoot-out on post.

She couldn't take a third call telling her Jamison had walked into danger again and would never be coming home.

Michele couldn't bear losing him. Better to guard her heart than to have it break again.

* * *

Jamison left the Logan home with Michele's words ricocheting through his mind. *"You made a mistake. You put yourself in danger. You walked into that ambush."*

Once he had ensured that the military police guards were in place and her neighborhood was being patrolled, Jamison drove back to CID headquarters.

Michele was right. He had failed tens months ago. He couldn't fail again. The stakes were too high.

"You'll never succeed." His father's voice rumbled through his head.

Jamison had to prove his dad wrong, but more important was the knowledge that if anything happened to Michele, Jamison would never be able to forgive himself.

She couldn't reconcile herself to what had happened to her brother. The anger and accusation in Michele's voice were outward signs of her long-term internal struggle. Would she ever be able to forgive herself?

Without a change of heart, she would never accept Jamison again. She had loved him once and had said as much tonight, but a terrible realization clamped down on Jamison's gut.

Sometimes love wasn't enough.

NINE

Tree frogs and cicadas sounded in the night. Jamison stood at the curb close to his car and eyed the brick façade of the Logan quarters. The light from the front porch spilled onto the walkway and the shrubbery that edged the house. Inside, a few lamps were on in the living room. Upstairs, where Michele slept, the house was dark.

He'd worked for hours on the investigation until his head ached and the muscles in his neck screamed for relief. Getting into his car, Jamison had driven back to check on Michele because he could find no rest until he knew she was safe.

The memory of her words stabbed at his heart. If only she could turn her problems over to the Lord and allow Him into her life. Ten months ago, she had gone to church with Jamison, and both of them had talked about wanting to put God first. Everything had changed after the shootout. When she'd run from Jamison, she'd run from her faith, as well.

Comfort her in her time of need, Lord. As the prayer left his mouth, one of the military policemen assigned to guard Mrs. Logan and her daughter walked around the corner of the house.

Jamison met him halfway. "How's it look in the rear?"

"Quiet, sir. Rogers and Yeoman are patrolling the woods to ensure that no one is lurking nearby. So far so good." He glanced at the house. "We need to find that guy and make sure he never strikes again."

Jamison agreed.

As the military policeman returned to his post, headlights cut through the darkness. Dawson's car pulled over to the curb. The special agent's limp seemed more pronounced when he exited his vehicle and walked along the sidewalk, the night air, no doubt, adding to his stiffness.

Jamison should have been the one injured instead of Dawson. The injury would have been easier to bear than being reminded of his own mistake each time he saw his friend.

When the wounded agent was coming out of surgery, Jamison had tried to express how he felt. Regrettably, he had choked on the words, and Dawson had never mentioned Jamison's attempt to ask forgiveness.

"We did some checking on the maintenance man," Dawson offered as he neared. "Danny Altman worked in Atlanta for a couple years after he got out of the army and only recently moved to the Fort Rickman area."

"Did you contact his old company?"

Dawson nodded. "He was a good worker, but with the downturn in the economy, the Atlanta firm had to cut back. They laid off a number of employees. He was one of them."

"What about the girlfriend's death?"

"Evidently, she was abusing prescription drugs and died of an overdose. The Atlanta P.D. interrogated the boyfriend, but he turned out to be clean."

"That doesn't mean he didn't have anything to do with the crimes on post."

Dawson shrugged. Even in the half-light from the streetlight, Jamison could see the question in the other man's eyes. "I didn't have any reason to hold him, but we'll keep our eyes on him and see what happens. If he's guilty, he won't like us getting in the middle of his life."

"I'd feel better if we restricted him from post."

"The man needs work."

"As long as that's all he's doing." Jamison didn't want Danny Altman anywhere near Michele.

He glanced up at her bedroom window, and his neck burned when he realized Dawson had followed his gaze.

"How is she?" Dawson asked.

"Struggling with a lot of things."

"Being the first at a crime scene can play with a person's mind. Double that by two and anyone would have problems."

"Mrs. Hughes's death brought back memories of her brother. Michele blames herself. That's hard to handle."

Dawson looked away and studied the sky. "Guilt's a funny thing. Once you take it on, it's almost impossible to release." He turned back to Jamison. "Asking forgiveness after the fact isn't always enough."

Jamison felt the weight he carried increase. Dawson was right. Guilt had a tight hold. Like a man-of-war that wraps tentacles around its victim, guilt's grasp has the same deadly sting.

"Look, Dawson—"

The sound of the front door opening made Jamison turn toward the brick quarters. Michele stood just inside the threshold.

Dawson patted Jamison's shoulder. "Looks like Michele wants to talk. I'm heading home for some shut-eye. Call me if anything comes up."

"Will do." Jamison stepped from the shadows and onto the sidewalk leading to the Logans' front stoop. Michele wore jeans and a print top that reminded him of sunshine and flowers.

As much as Jamison needed to think of Michele as a witness in an investigation, the emotions welling up within him were anything but professional. The late hour, the almost full moon, the sounds of the peaceful night and a beautiful woman waiting for him at the front door added to the anticipation teasing through his gut.

He hastened up the stairs, staring into her eyes. "Everything okay inside?"

She looked tired with puffy cheeks as if she had spent the better part of the night crying. His heart went out to her, wishing she would step outside so he could wrap her in his arms.

The only thing that kept him from reaching for her was the detail of soldiers pulling surveillance. Jamison would never allow them to see the way he really felt about the colonel's daughter.

Glancing past Michele, he saw Mrs. Logan in the dining room. She was arranging a pot of coffee and a plate of cookies on the table.

Michele hesitated a moment before she spoke. "I…I said too much earlier."

"It's okay. I wanted to know how you felt." He rubbed his finger across her cheek. "I'll always want to know."

She stepped onto the porch and wrapped her arms around her waist. A gentle breeze ruffled her hair and wafted a swirl of her sweet-smelling perfume to tempt him.

"Chilly?" he asked, wanting any excuse to touch her shoulder and pull her closer.

"The breeze feels good. The house seemed stuffy. Mother tries to conserve energy and turns the air conditioner thermostat down at night."

"I thought both of you were sound asleep."

She shook her head, her eyes filled with sadness. "Mother and Erica Grayson have been calling back and forth, discussing ways to help Yolanda's husband and his children."

"Mrs. Hughes's sister-in-law arrived today."

"That's right. She's trying to arrange a leave of absence from her job so she can stay indefinitely. The family will move temporarily into the furnished quarters reserved for visiting VIPs. The commanding general said he'll authorize anything they need."

Jamison nodded. "A crew is cleaning their old quarters, although I'm not sure if Major Hughes will want to move his family back in."

"Curtis can decide that after the funeral. He plans to have a memorial service at the Main Post Chapel when he and the children return from Missouri."

"Your mother talked to him?"

"After he broke the news to the children on Skype. He wanted to see their sweet faces and measure their reactions. The Graysons and his sister-in-law were sitting with the children when he told them. He said they needed to be strong and that they'd be together as soon as he got home."

Her voice hitched, and she blinked back tears. "Yolanda had miscarried a few years back. He said their mama was with their little brother now."

Jamison's throat thickened. "The whole family must be devastated, but it's got to be so hard on the children."

"Erica said they were brave kids and told their dad to be careful and stay safe. She doesn't think they understand everything at this point. They're in shock, in another home. When they disconnected, they told her they didn't want their dad to worry about them."

"Good kids, huh?"

"Army brats are usually pretty resilient. Moving from

place to place, always having to make new friends, they get used to new areas, even foreign countries. But this is tough."

Michele glanced momentarily into the night. "Can you imagine how often the children will wonder if they could have done something to have changed the events that day? If they hadn't gone to the Graysons' and had stayed home to help their mom that night, or if their dad hadn't been deployed or in the military? All those questions will run through their heads."

"Michele, that's what you've done with your brother's death. You keep thinking 'what if.' What if you hadn't helped with the relief effort? What if you had visited Lance that weekend? Talk to your mother. You've got to share your feelings with her before you can heal."

A tear ran down Michele's cheek. She pushed open the door.

He reached for her. "Don't run away."

"I'm not running. Not this time. But it's late, and I'm tired. You need sleep and so do I."

Before he could respond, Michele entered the house and raced up the stairs.

Mrs. Logan peered outside and saw him standing there, unable to speak, his throat still thick from the thought of the Hughes children and the window Michele had opened to reveal her own inner turmoil.

"I've perked a pot of coffee and put out cookies. Help yourself, Jamison, and have the other men get something, as well."

He held up his hand. "Nothing for me, ma'am, but I'll tell the men."

Backing down the steps, he glanced up at Michele's window. The light from the hallway shone into her room. She had pulled back the curtain and stood, looking down at him, never realizing Jamison could see her outlined against the faint glow from the hallway.

She was grieving for Yolanda but also for her brother. And Jamison? He was still grieving for Michele.

TEN

Michele woke the next morning with a dull headache and the sniffles. She felt achy and sore as if she'd battled some unseen foe all night. Truth was, she had slept little and had been barraged with images of Yolanda's and Alice's battered bodies.

Jamison's face had traveled through her thoughts, as well. His smile of old had been replaced with a perpetual look of determination that revealed his own personal struggle to find the killer. In endless waves of terror, the knife, the blood, the carnage had all visited her in the night.

Wiping her hand over her face, she pulled herself from the bed and padded toward the window. Low cloud cover hid the sun and cast the day in a dirty gray that felt as heavy as her spirits.

Once upon a time, she had been strong and self-reliant. Now she doubted her own ability, her resolve and even her desire to do the right thing. Everything inside her was mixed together in a chaos that got darker with every turn.

She peered around the curtain at the yard below. Two military policemen stood on the sidewalk. Even without checking, she knew two more would be guarding the house in the rear.

Straining to glance down the street, she failed to see

Jamison's car. He must have left sometime in the night. No reason for him to stay round the clock. He needed rest and time off. Surely he had a life outside of work. Maybe even a new girlfriend, although the thought of him with another woman soured her stomach and turned the gray day even darker.

Coffee would clear her mind. Michele headed to the kitchen and was soon pouring the first cup from the pot she brewed. The rich aroma filled the kitchen and stamped normalcy on the new day.

Except nothing was normal about this Thursday.

"Morning, honey." Her mother stepped into the breakfast area and pulled a cup from the cupboard. "Coffee smells good."

"I didn't hear you come down the stairs."

"That's because I was in the living room. I couldn't sleep and got up at the first light of dawn. I've been reading my devotionals and writing in my journal. Somehow it's helped."

Michele took another long sip from her cup. There was no reason to upset her mother by sharing her own thoughts on God.

"I walked by your door a number of times." Her mother raised her brow. "You were tossing and turning most of the night."

Michele tried to smile. Her mother had an innate ability to sense whether her daughter had had a good night's sleep. "I couldn't seem to get comfortable. The last time I looked at the clock, it was 4:00 a.m. I must have dozed off by the time you came downstairs. I kept thinking about Alice. Any news on her condition?"

"Only that she's still in ICU and critical." Roberta poured coffee into her cup. "Your father called this morning. The planes are on the tarmac. He'll let me know once they board."

Michele thought of his smile and twinkling eyes and wanted him home safely. Then she thought of Jamison, and her cheeks burned.

"Something wrong, dear? You look a little flushed." Her mother touched her forehead with the back of her hand. "Do you have a fever?"

"It's probably the coffee."

"I'm going to shower. Chaplain Grant scheduled the prayer service for 11:00 a.m."

Michele refilled her cup and followed her mother upstairs. When she heard the shower running, she opened the drawer on her dresser. Her eyes fell on the Bible Lance had given her. She touched the leather cover and sighed.

As much as she wanted to stay home this morning, she didn't want to have to answer her mother's probing questions. Michele had never shared her change of heart concerning faith, a faith her parents had hoped to instill in both their children.

The lessons had found a home in Lance. If he hadn't been snatched away so young, they might also have taken hold in Michele. As it was, she couldn't trust a God who disregarded the well-being of His children.

Her own internal struggle continued as she walked into the Main Post Chapel and took her seat in the pew next to her mother. At least they were sitting by the aisle. If she needed to excuse herself from the service, she could do so without disrupting anyone.

Glancing around, Michele saw many of the brigade wives and family members. The choir leader stood and invited the congregation to do likewise. He led them in a poignant hymn that called upon the Lord to come to the aid of His people in their need.

As much as Michele wanted to sing, the words stuck in her throat. Her mother didn't seem to notice, nor did she see how Michele worried her fingers and had to hold herself in check not to run from the assembly when the chaplain stepped to the pulpit.

Her head pounded even more as she tried to ignore his words about God's loving providence. Everything inside her cried out against the hypocrisy of the teaching. She started to rise, but someone slipped into the pew next to her, blocking her escape.

Frustrated, she closed her eyes and sat back, silently counting to ten before she glanced at the newcomer.

Jamison.

Her heart accelerated.

He crooked a smile and leaned close. "Thanks for saving me a seat."

She clasped her hands together in an attempt to appear in control, all the while wanting to race out of the church and away from a God she didn't trust and a man who made her think back to when life was good.

Her mother glanced around Michele and smiled. "Morning, Jamison."

"Nice to see you, ma'am," he whispered.

"Any news on Alice?"

"Her condition hasn't changed."

"What are you doing here?" Michele said out of the side of her mouth, once her mother turned her attention back to the service. Michele kept her voice low so only Jamison could hear.

"Giving honor to God."

"I mean, why are you sitting next to me?"

"I'm protecting you."

She crossed her legs and wrapped her arms over her chest, trying to tune out the chaplain's message.

Instead she was tuning in Jamison and the aftershave he wore and the dark sports coat and gray slacks and blue tie that made his ruddy complexion even more appealing. He might be clean shaven and showered, but the creases at the corners of his eyes confirmed he hadn't taken her advice about getting sleep.

Michele kept her guard up. The last time she'd been in church with Jamison had been shortly before he and Dawson had walked into the cross fire. More than a year earlier, Lance had died after she had begun to test the gospel message. Every time she got close to God, He raised the price of faith.

She needed to block out the chaplain's words. If she began to believe again, someone else might be taken from her. Michele looked at Jamison, knowing he was the likely target.

Jamison settled into the pew and enjoyed Michele's closeness. Her immediate reaction had been to bristle when he sat down. Before long, she'd relaxed and even smiled at him as they'd joined in singing one of the hymns.

The service concluded too quickly in his opinion, and once outside, his cell vibrated. He checked caller ID. Dawson.

"I've gotta go," he said to Michele.

She looked disappointed. A good sign.

"You'll be at the barracks later today?" he asked.

She nodded.

"Corporal McGrunner will be your escort."

"He followed us here."

"Good. He'll follow you home, too." With a nod to Mrs. Logan, he left Michele and headed to his car, opening his cell phone on the way.

"Yeah, Dawson, what's up?"

"The chief called a briefing."

"What time?"

"As soon as you can get here."

"Anything new I should know about?" Jamison asked as he settled behind the wheel and pulled out of the church parking lot.

"Only that the commanding general wants the killer in custody, and he's putting pressure to bear on the chief, who will, no doubt, pass the pressure on to us."

"That's the way the army works."

"Unfortunately. I got in touch with the cemetery director. Sergeant Brandon Carmichael's grave site is located near the central oak tree."

"Bingo. Tell me his daddy drives a black car with tinted windows and I'll be happy."

"A white SUV. I sent a couple of our men to talk to Mr. Carmichael. He's out of town. The new Mrs. Carmichael was cooperative. According to her, Carmichael left Freemont last Sunday on a weeklong fishing trip with some of his old pals. He wasn't in town yesterday, so he didn't visit the cemetery. In fact, he rarely goes to his son's grave site. She says it's too painful."

Mrs. Logan could probably relate.

"What about Greg Yates?" Jamison asked.

"He showed up with his son in tow. The kid's nineteen and flew into Atlanta on Tuesday night."

"Where's he usually live?"

"With his mother in Texas. Yates said he got a surprise call from his son the afternoon of the potluck and had to hustle to Atlanta before the plane landed, only the storms rolled in. Flights were delayed, and once the son finally arrived, it was late. They got a motel room and took in a Braves game the next day."

"And they drove back to Freemont last night."

"Roger that."

"Did you ask him about the possible divorce?"

"He blames it on lack of communication, and hopes his wife will consider counseling. Yates said he'll do anything to save his marriage."

Jamison glanced at his watch. "Tell the chief I'm on the way."

Nothing new came out of the very lengthy meeting with Wilson except the reminder of the need to wrap up the investigation as soon as possible. Finding Mrs. Hughes's killer was key, not that the chief needed to tell anyone. The entire CID and military police force were committed to finding the perpetrator and bringing him to justice. After the briefing, Jamison completed a few additional tasks that needed his attention and that Wilson had requested.

By the time he left CID headquarters, the day was well spent. He had wanted to be with Michele earlier, but what he wanted had to take a backseat to the job that needed to get done. At least McGrunner was with her, keeping watch, ensuring that she and Mrs. Logan were safe.

Jamison drove to the brigade headquarters. Double-timing inside, he flashed his CID identification to a staff sergeant standing near the door. "Mrs. Logan and some of the wives are working in the area."

"Yes, sir." The sergeant pointed through a nearby window to a building one block south of the headquarters. "You can see their cars from here."

With a nod of thanks, Jamison hustled outside and moved his own vehicle to the front of the barracks the sergeant had indicated. Getting out of his car, he spied Corporal McGrunner carrying a large potted plant.

The military policeman shifted the greenery to his left hand and saluted with his right. "Sir, Mrs. Logan and her daughter are on the third floor in the Day Room. The florist donated plants, and the ladies are making welcome-home bags for all the soldiers."

"Any sign of trouble?"

"No, sir. Except Mrs. Logan needed help bringing in the plants."

"Isn't the florist around?"

"He's upstairs arranging some of the flowers."

"Flowers in the Day Room?"

McGrunner nodded. "He donated potted plants and a few cut arrangements. Mrs. Logan says he's been extremely generous."

Jamison harrumphed. He doubted the male soldiers cared about flowers, but the few female soldiers in the unit would probably appreciate the florist's generosity.

Memo to self. If he ever fell in love again, he'd send flowers. Lots of flowers on a regular basis.

Jamison headed for the stairwell and hurried upstairs. On the third floor, he turned right and followed the sound of voices.

Approaching an open door, he glanced inside. Michele stood at the foot of a single bed, straightening the end of the blanket.

"Need some help?"

She looked up, startled.

"Sorry to frighten you." The room smelled like lemon furniture polish. He noticed a man standing near the corner, holding a dust cloth. Dressed in civilian clothes, he was tall with a muscular build. Mid-forties.

"Have you met Greg Yates?" Michele asked. "His wife is in the brigade."

"Special Agent Steele." Jamison extended his hand, which Yates shook with a firm grasp.

Michele stepped toward the door. "Mother's in the Day Room, if you need to talk to her. I'm headed that way."

Jamison followed Michele into the hallway. She glanced at him over her shoulder. "You had a phone call after the service this morning. Did something happen?"

"Information came in on Carmichael."

"The soldier who was killed in Iraq?"

"That's right. Do you have any idea how old the man at the cemetery might have been?"

"He was too far away to tell.

"Gray hair? Stooped shoulders? Perhaps a hesitation in his gait?"

"He appeared strong and healthy."

After making the bed in a second room, Jamison and Michele headed to the Day Room, where Greg had joined a group of wives, stuffing individually wrapped baked goods into plastic bags.

Mrs. Logan had a wide smile on her face. "We could use your help, Jamison." She pointed to the florist. "Teddy's donated some lovely plants that need to be brought into the building, if you can lend a hand."

Teddy waved from the desk where he was adding American flags and red, white and blue bows to three large floral arrangements.

McGrunner entered the Day Room. He placed the plant he carried on the table where Teddy worked and smiled. "Follow me, sir."

Jamison turned to the major's husband. "You want to lend a hand, Mr. Yates?"

The guy shook his head. "No can do. Bad back."

Yet he appeared bulked up as if he pumped iron on a regular schedule.

Shrugging out of his sports coat, Jamison hung it over the back of a chair and followed McGrunner down the stairs. On the first floor, he grabbed a cart from a utility closet. Unloading the remaining plants onto the cart, they pushed them toward the inside stairwell and, from there, carried them up the stairs.

Michele wasn't in the Day Room when he returned. "Where's your daughter?" Jamison asked Mrs. Logan.

"She and Teddy took a couple of flower arrangements to one of the other floors."

Leaving McGrunner to bring up the rest of the plants, Jamison went in search of Michele.

The overhead lights were out at the rear of the building, sending shadows to darken the hallway. Turning a corner, he spied Teddy walking toward him.

"Where's Miss Logan?"

"Giving directions to a soda distributor named Perkins. He couldn't find the soft drink machines."

Jamison hadn't seen any distributor's truck parked out front.

"Where'd they go?"

"Downstairs." Teddy pointed over his shoulder. "End of the hall, then left. The machines are directly below, on the second floor."

The muscles in Jamison's shoulders tightened as he raced to the end of the hallway. Taking the steps two at a time, he called Michele's name and pushed through the fire door into the unlit second floor. "Michele?"

Silence.

Then a gasp. A scuffling sound followed.

"Michele?" He turned the corner, ready to confront anyone or anything doing her harm.

She stood in a narrow room surrounded by soda dispensing machines. Hand at her throat, she stared at a man crouched on his hands and knees in the corner.

"Step toward me, Michele."

She looked surprised. "What?"

"Step away from the man. Now."

"I'm okay. Really. It was a mouse."

Jamison frowned. "What?"

Michele pointed to where the man was peering under one of the vending machines. "I was showing Mr. Perkins the soft drink machines when a mouse ran across the floor."

"Looks like he's disappeared." Perkins stood. "You'd better report it. Someone needs to set a trap and catch the critter."

He glanced at the SIG Sauer on Jamison's hip. "Then again, you could shoot him."

The guy wore navy chinos and a polo shirt. Solid build, probably weighed somewhere between two-ten and two-twenty. Pudgy hands, well callused.

Jamison zeroed in on the scratch marks around his wrists and lower arms.

"Michele, go back to the Day Room."

"What?"

Why did she always have to question him when he was trying to keep her safe?

"Go upstairs to the third floor and rejoin the other women."

She narrowed her gaze. "I don't understand."

"Michele, please—" He jerked his head toward the door. "Upstairs. Now. Rejoin the other ladies."

Finally, she did as he had asked. Jamison was relieved when her footfalls sounded going up the stairs.

"I'm Special Agent Steele, CID." Jamison flashed his identification. "I'd like to see the paperwork authorizing you to be on post."

Perkins rolled his eyes. "You've got to be kidding."

"No, sir. I need your authorization."

Despite his attitude, the distributor pulled the papers from his pocket.

Pete Perkins. Freemont address.

"You want to tell me what you're doing here, Mr. Perkins?"

He spread his hands and took a step toward Jamison.

"Stay where you are, sir."

The guy stopped, brows raised. "Look, I don't want to cause any problem."

"Where's your truck?"

"Out back. I came in through the rear door."

"Aren't you supposed to wear a uniform shirt with your company's logo?"

"I'm not on the clock. I work for my brother-in-law and was helping him out. The machines need to be filled before the brigade returns."

"How'd you get those scratches on your arm?"

The guy furrowed his brow. "What are you talking about?"

"Two women were attacked on post."

His eyes widened. "You think I was involved?"

"You can explain everything at CID headquarters."

"That's ridiculous."

"Is it? Then I suggest you explain about the scratches."

The guy fisted his hands and shoved out his chest. "Who do you think you are?"

"As I mentioned earlier, I'm a special agent with the CID, and I'm hauling you into CID headquarters unless you explain why you're so agitated about answering a few questions."

The guy cursed.

Jamison pointed to the hallway. "After you, Mr. Perkins."

As they walked from the building into the late afternoon, Corporal McGrunner approached Jamison. "Problem, sir?"

"Take Mr. Perkins back to headquarters. I'll contact Special Agent Timmons and let him know you're bringing him in for questioning.

"Roger that, sir."

Perkins, grumbling under his breath, climbed into the rear of the military police sedan. As McGrunner pulled away from the barracks, Perkins stared at Jamison out the rear window.

Sensing someone behind him, Jamison turned and saw Michele standing in the doorway of the barracks. The florist stood beside her, along with Mrs. Logan.

"We're finished," Michele said as they stepped outside. She glanced at the military police sedan heading away from the building. "Corporal McGrunner drove us here, but he seems to be busy. Any chance you could give us a ride home?"

"Of course."

Their fingers brushed together as she handed Jamison his jacket. "You left this in the Day Room."

Her touch threw him off-kilter. He didn't need to stare into her questioning blue eyes to know she thought he'd overreacted upstairs.

Maybe he had. But Mr. Perkins had balked at answering a few questions. With a killer on the loose, anything and anyone suspect had to be questioned. The CID needed to know if Perkins had something to hide.

The florist waved as he ambled toward his truck. "See you folks tomorrow at the airport."

Michele waved back. "Thanks, Teddy."

Jamison shrugged into his jacket. "After I drive you home, I want to ensure that there's enough security around your quarters before I head to the hospital to check on Mrs. Rossi."

He held open the passenger and rear doors. Mrs. Logan

climbed into the backseat, leaving the front for Michele. Jamison strengthened his resolve to remain unaffected by the colonel's daughter, knowing after the investigation was over, he wouldn't see Michele again.

ELEVEN

Michele glanced over her shoulder to where her mother sat in the rear seat of Jamison's car. "Check your cell, Mother. Dad may have phoned."

"I just did, dear. No messages and no new calls."

Michele sighed. "I thought the brigade would have been on board the plane by now."

"Your father will do everything in his power to let us know when they're ready to take off."

"Do you think something happened?" Michele couldn't help expressing the concern that bubbled up inside her.

"I'm sure he's fine." Jamison's voice was filled with understanding. "Hurry up and wait is the army way of life."

"My dad uses that same phrase, but its hard being the one at home who's watching the clock."

"The word I got was that everything was on schedule." He pulled out his cell. "I'll call the rear detachment."

"Roger that," he said at the conclusion of the rather terse conversation with the duty officer.

Jamison turned to Michele. "Good news. The planes are airborne. They had an hour delay in boarding, but they're on their way home."

Michele looked back at her mother. "Why didn't Dad let us know?"

"Your father has a lot to take care of, dear. He probably ran out of time before takeoff. I'm sure he'll phone when they land to refuel."

"He's as anxious as you are to get the brigade back to Fort Rickman," Jamison offered along with a warm smile.

He was right. As a brigade commander, her father would put his soldiers' needs first. They'd been deployed for a year and were eager to get back to their families. The fact that two wives in the unit had been brutally attacked would make them even more anxious to be reunited with their loved ones.

In a way, Michele felt guilty for enjoying the comforts of home when so many gave up so much in order to serve their country. Recently, she had lived with a constant dread that something would happen to her dad. As she waited for news of his departure, her concerns had grown even more pronounced. She should be feeling relief, knowing he was airborne, but Michele still worried and needed something to occupy her thoughts and her time.

She turned to Jamison. "I'd like to go to the hospital with you when you check on Alice." Michele glanced over her shoulder. "You'll be all right while I'm gone, won't you, Mother?"

"Of course." Roberta shifted in her seat. "Jamison, how long will you keep the guard stationed outside Alice's hospital room? Corporal McGrunner said someone is with her at all times."

"Until we capture the killer. If he learns Mrs. Rossi is alive, he may try to finish the job. I want to make sure we find him before he does more harm."

He glanced at Michele. "You need to be especially careful. Tell the military police assigned to guard your house when you're leaving. Don't go any place without letting me know, either."

She wrapped her arms around her waist. "You're starting to scare me."

"I'm trying to ensure that you don't do something foolish."

"Like drive away from McGrunner when he's tied up in a traffic jam?"

Jamison nodded. "Exactly."

"In my own defense, if I had waited any longer, I wouldn't have gotten to Alice in time."

"And if your mother hadn't pounded on the door, we wouldn't be having this conversation." Jamison's voice was chillingly cold and devoid of inflection.

If he was trying to upset Michele, he was succeeding. She hadn't felt afraid for herself after Yolanda's death. She'd been more concerned about the other wives. But coming face-to-face with the killer and knowing he might finish the job he'd started sent pinpricks of fear tingling along her spine.

"I'll make sure I stay close to my military police guards until you find the killer."

Jamison glanced in the rearview mirror. "That goes for you, too, Mrs. Logan. Watch yourself at all times. Check before you open the door. Don't take walks alone or visit one of the wives without an MP escort."

"Michele and I will follow the rules, Jamison. But I worry about the wives who aren't getting the VIP treatment."

"I understand your concern, ma'am. As I told you earlier, we've increased law enforcement's presence on post and are patrolling the housing areas. The neighborhood watch programs are working. If anyone spots something suspicious in the housing areas, they're calling CID headquarters or the military police. We've been able to apprehend a number of people who haven't had a good reason to be on Fort Rickman."

"But you don't have a suspect."

"Not yet, but with the number of tips coming in, we're optimistic about finding the killer soon."

"That would certainly be an answered prayer," Mrs. Logan said with a sigh.

"Yes, ma'am."

Once again, Michele felt Jamison's gaze. She shifted away from him and looked out the window. Too many thoughts circled through her head, thoughts of her father and his men already in the air and the families counting down the hours and minutes until they would be reunited.

She thought of Alice's husband frantic to be at his wife's bedside and Major Hughes, who needed to reunite with his children. Knowing Yolanda wouldn't be at the airfield to greet him put an even darker reality on the rapidly descending twilight outside the car.

Everything Jamison had said was true. Michele needed to be careful, but so did the other women on post. No matter what the CID and military police hoped would happen in the upcoming hours, everyone knew the killer could strike again.

Jamison would keep her safe, but a question kept circling through her mind that was more troubling than any concerns about her own well-being.

Who would protect Jamison?

Silence filled the car as Jamison turned into the Logans' housing area. In the rear seat, Mrs. Logan seemed in her own world. She was probably thinking of the planeload of men flying back to Fort Rickman and the commander she was eager to have home.

If body language meant anything, Michele had distanced herself from Jamison and was wrapped in her own struggle, which he wouldn't attempt to understand. Hopefully, her outlook would improve when Colonel Logan was safe at home. Key word: safe.

Jamison mentally ticked off the plans he had put in place for the homecoming reunion at the airfield. Security would be as tight as a steel drum. The family members would wait in the terminal where military police and CID could protect them. The chaplain would be standing by to take Major Hughes to his children. Another escort would transport Sergeant Rossi to the hospital, where he could be reunited with his wife.

Dawson was encouraged by the recent influx of phone tips, and Jamison had passed on that optimism to Mrs. Logan when she had asked about the investigation. The truth was the killer was still on the loose.

As much as Perkins's attitude concerned Jamison, the soda distributor probably wasn't involved. Hauling him into the CID headquarters was a precautionary measure, which would also help to adjust his outlook. Anyone coming onto Fort Rickman needed to realize the military followed a strict set of rules that everyone, even civilians, needed to follow.

Once again, he glanced at Michele, who still found the outside world more intriguing than what went on inside the car. If only he could read her mind. Fact was, he wasn't sure of anything concerning Michele right now. Ten months ago, he had thought they were good together.

His mistake. A big mistake that had cost him dearly.

Luckily, he was wiser and stronger now.

When the killer was brought to justice, Michele would return to Atlanta, and Jamison would move on with his life. The thought should provide welcome relief. Instead all Jamison could think of was the sense of emptiness he would feel when Michele left him again.

TWELVE

The hospital smelled like a mix of cleaning products and rubbing alcohol as Michele stepped into the elevator ahead of Jamison. He pushed the button, then placed his hand on her back and nudged her forward when the door opened on the third floor.

Any other time, she might have balked at his attempt to guide her toward the Intensive Care Unit. This evening, she found the warmth of his hand splayed across her back reassuring.

Not that she was ready to open the door they had closed months ago. Correction. The door *she* had closed. Jamison hadn't run after her, but he had phoned her several times, although she had never answered his calls.

Fear had kept her from talking to him, fear of hearing his voice and knowing how quickly she might run back to Fort Rickman. She couldn't endure life always wondering if the man she loved would be coming home at night.

Walking next to Jamison at this moment brought another thought to mind: the heady possibility of what their future could be if only he would leave the army and law enforcement.

Of course, she knew that would be asking more than he was willing to give. The military and his job defined who he was. Better to maintain their current status quo than to try to mend a relationship that could never be fixed.

Entering the ICU, she and Jamison approached the nurses' desk. He held out his identification to the receptionist who pointed out Alice's room.

"Mrs. Rossi's condition has improved ever so slightly, but she's not strong enough to answer questions."

Jamison nodded. "I just need to talk to the military policeman guarding her."

The MP sat outside Alice's door. He had a ruddy complexion, auburn hair and green eyes that reflected the warm smile covering his face. The name tag on his uniform read Riley.

"Sir." He stood as they neared and nodded to Jamison before he looked at Michele. "Ma'am."

"How's everything going, Corporal?" Jamison asked.

"Fine, sir. The nurses are on top of things. I overheard them saying Mrs. Rossi is somewhat better."

"Anyone other than the nurses trying to gain access to her room?"

"A couple folks from the lab were here earlier to draw blood. A guy from respiratory therapy gave her a breathing treatment. No one else has been around."

As the two men talked, Michele slipped into the small ICU room. Alice's face looked pasty white against the bleached cotton bedding. Her neck was bandaged and her eyes were closed and lined with deep, dark circles. Her chest rose and fell under the sheet as oxygen entered her lungs through a nasal cannula.

Michele stepped closer. For half a heartbeat, she considered offering a prayer for the sweet lady who needed to survive, and for her husband, flying home from the war zone. Sergeant Rossi had survived enemy attacks and scud missiles that blasted through their forward operating base without being harmed. Hard to believe his wife had been the one injured during his deployment.

Hearing footsteps, Michele turned as Jamison entered the room and stopped at the foot of the bed. His face revealed his own concern as to whether Alice would survive her injuries.

Before Michele could consider what she was asking, the words tumbled from her mouth. "Will…will you say a prayer?"

Although her voice had only been a whisper, Jamison raised his gaze, his eyes locking on hers. She had the sense that he could see into the depths of her being. Maybe he understood her fear of losing another person about whom she cared.

Jamison raised his brow. "Is that something you want me to do?"

Glancing down at the unresponsive patient, Michele nodded. "I think it's what Alice would want."

Jamison's voice was husky when he finally spoke. "Father, we ask for protection and healing for Mrs. Rossi. See the love in her heart and the future You have planned for her. Let all things work together for her good."

"Amen," Michele whispered.

Overcome with sadness, she walked back into the hallway, needing to distance herself from the machines keeping Alice alive and from the prayer she had asked Jamison to say. What had caused her to seek God's mercy when the doctors and nurses and all the advances of medical science were working together to save Alice's life?

Michele knew better than to rely on the Lord or His healing love. She wanted to hear about Alice's improved test results, like her oxygen level and white blood cell count. Drugs and doctors and hospital personnel would bring Alice through, not Jamison's prayer.

"Michele, wait," he called after her.

She pointed to the water fountain in the alcove. "I'm getting a drink." Her throat burned and her mouth was as dry as cardboard. A heavy weight sat on her chest, and hot tears stung her eyes. If she gave in to her emotions, she would break down and cry, and she had shed too many tears already.

Resolved to maintain her control, she glanced back at Jamison. He was saying something to the military guard.

A phone rang at the nurses' desk. The ICU clerk answered the call and motioned to a male aide.

"Mrs. Rossi's doctor ordered a scan. Take her down on the back elevator. The MP needs to go with you."

A lump formed in Michele's throat. Seeing Alice brought back the terror she had felt last night.

Michele's knees went weak, and air rushed from her lungs. The memory of the explosive pain from the stun gun returned and made her muscles spasm as if it were happening again. She saw the killer hovering over her, the knife in his hand.

Unable to face the images that ran through her mind, Michele raced along the hallway.

Jamison called her name, but she couldn't turn back.

Just as before, Michele needed to leave Fort Rickman and everything that had happened. Then she realized leaving the post would mean she had to leave Jamison, as well.

Jamison found Michele near the elevator, arms wrapped protectively around her waist. Tears swam in her eyes, and her head rested against the cool tile wall.

"What's happening to me?"

He rubbed his hand over her shoulder. "You've been through a lot, Michele."

"I want to be strong, but I keep seeing the killer. What

he did to Yolanda and then Alice. I'll never get those images out of my mind."

She bit her lip. "You probably think I need to see a shrink."

"What you need is a good night's sleep. You look exhausted."

"I could say the same about you."

He wrapped his arm around her and pulled her close. "You were attacked and almost run over. Plus, you've lost a friend and don't know if another one will survive. That's a lot to carry." She smelled fresh like flowers and was just as soft as he remembered.

Holding Michele brought back memories he had tried to forget, like the sense of completeness that swept over him whenever she was in his arms. Running away from him had been a mistake, but he couldn't tell her that, especially now. If there was any hope for them in the future, she had to come to that conclusion on her own. All he could do was keep her safe until she realized that love sometimes was hard, but always worth the effort.

Feeling the tension in her shoulders, he rubbed his hand along her back. "Your dad's on his way home. Once he arrives, you can be a family again. Everything will be better then."

She edged back and looked up into his eyes. "You…you don't understand. Without Lance, we'll never be a family."

Would she ever get over her brother's death?

"Oh, honey." He pulled her closer. "Life is filled with joy and pain. We have to accept both."

"But my father—"

"He'll be home tomorrow. All you have to do is get through the night."

She sniffed. "But…"

He shook his head. "No buts. I'll be close by if you need me."

A heavy weight settled on Jamison's heart as he thought of what could be between them and the reality of what they had instead.

No matter how much he wanted to reconcile with the past, Jamison and Michele stood on opposite sides of a huge divide that seemed impossible to traverse. His love hadn't been enough for her to stay with him ten months ago. He doubted much had changed, except for his own desire to have her back in his life.

He ushered her toward the elevator and past a number of people on the first floor as they made their way toward the hospital's main entrance.

Always concerned about Michele's safety, Jamison scanned the lobby. A few people were milling around the main information desk, probably requesting room numbers for patients they planned to visit.

His gaze swept to the double glass doors that opened into the emergency room. A woman sat in the E.R. waiting area, head in her hands. A man huddled close by, rubbing her back. Other folks waited to be seen. A hospital security guard stood by the receptionist's desk, arms crossed over his chest. Behind the tall counter, a young clerk chatted with someone on the phone.

Everything looked normal. Nothing to worry about.

The tension in Jamison's neck began to subside. He pulled in a deep breath, but before he could exhale, the public address system screeched to life.

"Code Silver. Third floor. ICU. Code Silver."

Jamison's gut turned to ice. Code Silver meant an active shooter was in the hospital.

He grabbed Michele's arm and herded her into the E.R.

waiting room, flashing his identification at the security guard.

"Lock down all the doors to the E.R.," he told the clerk. "Don't let anyone in or out until you hear from me. Call the military police. Ensure that they know about the code, and get backup."

He motioned for Michele and the patients in the waiting room to hide behind the tall, wraparound counter. "Stay down. You'll be protected by the desk. An accomplice might be outside. Don't leave the E.R."

Fear flashed from Michele's eyes. "It's Alice, isn't it?"

"I don't know, honey, but don't move until an all clear comes over the PA system." He tapped the security guard's shoulder. "Come with me."

The two raced into the lobby. Jamison glanced back to ensure that the clerk had closed and locked the doors behind them.

Ignoring the elevator, Jamison opted for the stairs and climbed at breakneck speed, pulling his weapon as he raced toward the danger. The guard followed, but his steps were labored, and he was gasping for air by the third floor.

Weapon at the ready, Jamison opened the door and stepped into pandemonium.

In one sweep, he saw it all.

His throat thickened. Alice lay sprawled across the transport gurney with a gunshot wound to her side. Corporal Riley was on the floor, unconscious and surrounded by a growing pool of blood.

A doctor reached for the portable defibrillator on the floor next to the guard. A nurse cut open his uniform.

"Clear." The doc lowered the paddles onto the MP's sunken chest.

Additional medical personnel raced forward.

"Get her to the O.R. stat!" someone shouted. Hands pushed Alice toward a second elevator.

Jamison raised his voice over the chaos. "Which way did the shooter go?"

Someone pointed to an exit at the end of the hall. "Back stairway. Two security guards ran after him. The guy's wearing a black ski mask."

Jamison raced forward, shoved on the door to the stairwell and flew down the steps. At the bottom landing, he pressed through the first-floor exit and rushed into the humid night. Two security men stood under a streetlight in the rear parking area. One raised a handheld radio to his ear.

Hearing Jamison approach, the other guard turned and shook his head. "He got away."

Jamison pulled out his cell to notify the CID. Anger and frustration boiled up within him. He wanted to scream with rage. The killer had struck again. Alice was alive but only barely, and Jamison had no idea if she or Riley would survive the new injuries.

Jamison had been close. Yet not close enough.

He thought of Michele holed up in the E.R. At least she was safe.

The killer had a gun and was on the run. One thing was certain. He would strike again.

Jamison had to ensure that Michele wasn't the next person he planned to kill.

THIRTEEN

Michele hunkered down behind the counter in the emergency room, fearful of what was happening upstairs in the ICU. Sirens sounded in the distance and grew steadily louder, crescendoing in a deafening scream as a caravan of squad cars screeched to the curb outside. Flashing lights spilled through the windows, bathing the E.R. in a strobe-like effect that made her dizzy and even more afraid for Jamison's safety.

Military police swarmed into the lobby and ran for the stairwell. Peering over the top of the desk, Michele saw Dawson Timmons race past.

"We'll be all right," she said, trying to calm the patients gathered around her.

"The shooter must be that serial killer on post," a man said.

Next to him, a woman cried softly. "He'll find us," she said, her voice edged with fear.

"The CID and military police have everything under control." At least, that's what Michele wanted to believe.

The woman sniffed. "How can you be so sure?"

Michele shoved a box of tissues into her hands. "I know the special agents working on this case. They've had a lot of leads. The killer will be apprehended."

A second woman stood up. "I need to get home to my husband. He'll be worried."

Michele gently touched her arm. "Wait until the all clear. A few more minutes won't make a difference." The woman hesitated and then sat back down.

Michele breathed a sigh of relief. One problem averted, although she understood the woman's concern about her loved one. Michele's mother was home. Hopefully, she was occupied with homecoming plans and wouldn't hear about the attack at the hospital.

The clerk, in her early twenties with long hair and a tiny nose ring, leaned toward Michele, her voice low. "Does your boyfriend work for the police?"

Boyfriend? Michele had to smile. Once upon a time, Jamison had been even more than that to her. "He's a CID agent on post. Criminal Investigation Division."

The girl looked confused.

"You didn't grow up in the military?" Michele asked.

"My dad runs the Laundromat in town."

A civilian who didn't know about the army. "CID agents handle felony crimes against military personnel and their family members."

"So he's working on the murder case?"

"That's right." Although if Michele had heard Jamison's boss correctly, Chief Wilson had put Dawson in charge of the investigation. Jamison's job was to keep her and her mother safe.

Tough duty, especially when Michele had been so careless at the cemetery yesterday. If she had kept her head up and her eyes wide open, she would have gotten off the road at the first sign of the approaching car. She also would have waited for Jamison before driving to Alice's house last night, although as she'd told him earlier, arriving any later could have proven fatal to her friend.

Michele rubbed her hands over her brow and rested the back of her head against the counter. No matter how much she wanted to be optimistic, she was worried about Jamison.

The clerk pulled her legs to her chest and placed her chin on her knees, eyes closed. The other people sat with their own thoughts. Michele checked her watch, wishing she'd hear something about what was happening on the third floor.

"Tell him thanks."

Michele glanced at the clerk. "Pardon?"

"Thank your boyfriend for me. He tried to protect all of us." Her thin lips twitched into a soulful smile. "You're probably used to all the good he does, but I don't know guys like that." She chewed on her lip. "Your boyfriend's a hero. A superhero."

Michele closed her eyes. The young clerk had Jamison pegged. He was a man who always reacted in the face of any danger. Superheroes survived in spite of insurmountable odds because of their special powers, but Jamison survived because he was good at what he did and because he cared enough to try. Michele hadn't recognized what this young girl had noticed immediately. Jamison was a very special agent.

Voices sounded in the lobby. Glancing over the counter, she saw Jamison talking to Dawson. Relief swept over her. At least tonight's danger had passed.

A car engine sounded outside. She glanced out the window on the way to open the doors, planning to throw her arms around Jamison. But when he stood in front of her, all she could see was his face, twisted in pain, and the smear of blood across his once-white shirt.

"What happened?" she asked, fearing the worst.

"It's Alice."

Michele's hand flew to her throat.

"She's in surgery." Jamison hesitated. "They...they don't expect her to live."

Michele wanted to be a superhero like Jamison, but too much had happened. Tears clouded her eyes, and her knees went weak. She felt herself falling, but instead of crashing to the floor, she fell into Jamison's strong arms.

"It's going to be okay, honey," he soothed, rubbing his hands over her back.

Even superheroes sometimes lied, if the truth was too hard to accept, and the truth about Alice was more than Michele could bear.

Lance.

Yolanda.

Now Alice.

Michele's father was flying home from a war zone, and a killer was stalking his next victim.

Who would he come after next?

Terror seized her.

Superhero or not, Jamison would always be in the line of fire.

As worried as Jamison was about Michele's physical safety, he was even more concerned about her emotional well-being. Leaving Dawson to wrap up things at the hospital, Jamison tucked her into the passenger seat of his car and glanced into the night sky.

Please, Lord, Michele has been through so much. Comfort her the way I wish I could and keep her safe.

He needed to take Michele home before something happened to her or to his heart. As far as she was concerned, they weren't good together. She had made that perfectly clear ten months ago, but tonight he didn't care about what had been, he cared about the present moment. At the moment, he wanted to wrap Michele in his arms and never let her go.

FOURTEEN

Even with Jamison at her side, Michele felt drained as she climbed the stairs to her front porch. He had spent much of the ride home on the phone with Dawson. Alice and the nice military policeman assigned to guard her were both in surgery. The doctors didn't offer much hope for either patient.

Jamison talked to the security detail at her parents' quarters and then followed her onto the porch. Rummaging in her handbag, she found her house key and dropped it into his outstretched hand. Always the gentleman, he unlocked the door, stepped aside for her to enter and then followed her into the foyer.

Michele had expected to hear chatter from the wives' group and was surprised to find the house empty except for her mother, who stepped from the living room.

"Hello, dear." She lowered her cheek toward Michele and accepted a kiss, then greeted Jamison with a welcoming smile.

"How's Alice?"

"She…" The words stuck in Michele's throat. Jamison took over, for which she was grateful, and brought her mother up to date on what had happened.

Hearing the news, Roberta put her head in her hands and moaned. "Oh, dear God, when will it end?"

"Not until the killer's apprehended." Jamison stated what they all knew to be true. If only the arrest would come about without additional loss of life or injury.

"There's been too much suffering." Roberta reached for the sturdy oak banister as if needing support. Her eyes reflected pain and struggle and many of the feelings that had bombarded Michele over the last two days.

Tonight, the tiny lines around Roberta's eyes seemed more pronounced. Her skin appeared less vibrant, and her shoulders drooped. Michele had always considered her mother young for her age, but the years and the circumstances appeared to be taking their toll.

Michele forced a smile. "Dad will be home in the morning. Everything will be better then."

Roberta glanced into the dining room.

Michele followed her gaze to the bouquet of flowers her father had been thoughtful enough to send. "The arrangement looks nice on the table, Mother."

Roberta nodded a bit too enthusiastically, all the while blinking back tears that swarmed her eyes.

"Are you all right?" Always the rock, her mother usually seemed unflappable. Tonight she appeared as broken as Michele had felt earlier.

"I'm fine." Which was what Michele had said so many times recently.

Studying her mother's drawn face, Michele saw beneath the capable army wife facade to a woman who tried to appear stronger than she was. Roberta squared her shoulders, but the expression she wore revealed her fragile interior.

"What's wrong, Mother?"

"There's something I need to tell you, dear."

As if sensing the importance of the moment, Jamison

cleared his throat. "If you don't mind, ma'am, I'll step into the kitchen and call CID headquarters."

Once he left, Roberta squeezed Michele's hand. "Some things have been troubling both of us that need to be brought to light."

Michele wasn't sure where her mother was headed.

"I rarely talk about Lance, and I know that upsets you. The truth is his death left a hole in my heart that's been hard to fill. Your father dealt with his own grief by throwing himself into his work. When I tried to talk to him about what I was feeling, he told me to be strong."

She pointed to the table. "That bouquet is his first attempt to let me know he understands what I've been going through these last two years."

Regret swept over Michele. She had been so wrong about her mother. "I…I thought you didn't want to talk about Lance."

"I wanted to, but I couldn't. Even looking at old photos or visiting the cemetery with you was more than I could handle. I forced myself to go on for you and for your father. You were traveling a lot for the insurance company and seemed fairly self-sufficient. Dad had his work. Most of all, I didn't want to be a burden."

"Which you could never be, Mother."

A door had cracked open, but Michele still hesitated. Some doors needed to remain closed.

Her mother raised her hand to her throat and fingered the collar of her blouse. "I know you feel responsible for Lance's death, but you made the right decision to help with the storm relief."

Bitter denial welled up within Michele. "But if I hadn't gone to the coast, Lance would have been on leave, showing me around his new post. He wouldn't have volunteered to take that mission."

"Your brother loved the military, and he loved to fly. Going up that day was his decision, Michele. You were *not* to blame."

"But—"

"We'll never know why God called Lance home, yet we have to trust he's with the Lord. Scripture tells us with God everything works together for good."

Michele still couldn't trust the Lord, but seeing her mother's pain and hearing the sincerity in her voice allowed Michele to finally accept the truth. Her mother didn't blame her for Lance's death, which lifted a weight she had carried for too long.

Roberta opened her arms, and Michele stepped into her mother's welcoming embrace, overwhelmed with a sense of homecoming. Tears filled her eyes, but they were joyful tears that washed away the struggle she'd had with her mother. Roberta's tears seemed equally cathartic, and mother and daughter cried freely.

Hearing the commotion, Jamison raced into the foyer. The look on his face said he had misinterpreted their reconciliation as something more threatening. "Are you all right?"

"We're fine," they both said in unison, which caused them to laugh and wipe their eyes and feel the strong mother-daughter bond that had been absent for too long.

Michele's heart nearly burst with love for her mother. An equally strong feeling swept over her as she smiled at Jamison, who had given them the privacy they needed to heal.

"I'm starving," Michele admitted, a bit light-headed but in a good way.

"I've got leftovers in the fridge." Roberta motioned Jamison toward the kitchen. "I know you must be hungry, too. Let's have something to eat."

Michele raised her hand to her neck, knowing she and her mother could now talk freely about her brother. "You go ahead. I'll join you in a minute."

Running upstairs, she opened her dresser drawer and removed the lid from the wooden box she kept near her Bible. Her eyes rested on the delicate silver cross Lance had given her. On the same chain, Michele had placed a silver heart charm that had been a gift from Jamison shortly after they'd started dating. He'd called the silver dangles her Cross My Heart necklace, a necklace she had taken off the day she left Fort Rickman.

Michele was beginning to believe she had been wrong to leave Jamison. Surely things would be different once he understood her fears about his safety.

Almost giddy, she started to laugh, then quickly sobered, thinking of Alice, fighting for her life, and the brigade flying home through the night.

Hearing Jamison's voice from the kitchen, Michele clasped the necklace around her neck. Jamison was a hero, just as the clerk at the hospital had said, but a killer was still on the loose, and anything could happen. Once again, she needed to guard her heart. Only this time, Michele wasn't sure if she could.

FIFTEEN

Jamison looked up as Michele entered the kitchen. His breath caught in his throat at her freshness and beauty. Not only had the exhaustion disappeared from her eyes, but her smile was bright and lit up the room and his weary spirit. From across the kitchen, he could feel the draw of her magnetism and would have pulled Michele into his arms if her mother hadn't been standing nearby.

While Michele had been upstairs, he had changed into a fresh white shirt he kept in his car. Mrs. Logan had arranged a baked ham and a number of salads on the table, along with a loaf of sliced French bread.

As she prepared the food, Jamison had called the hospital. Alice remained in surgery. The MP had been moved into the recovery room but was still in serious condition.

"Help yourself." Mrs. Logan pulled plates from the cabinet and placed them on the table. "Coffee or cola?"

"Coffee sounds great." Jamison accepted a steaming mug and waited until Michele had her food before he made a ham sandwich and heaped the salads on his plate.

Once they had all settled into chairs around the kitchen table, Michele nudged his arm. "Would you offer thanks?"

Taken aback by the request, he was equally surprised to see the Cross My Heart necklace around her neck. Michele's talk with her mother seemed to have healed not only their relationship but also Michele's attitude toward the Lord. Overcome with relief, he wanted to cheer, but with both women waiting for the blessing, he rationalized giving thanks was a better way to handle his exuberance.

Following dinner, Michele refilled his mug and poured coffee for herself and her mother. "Any news from Dad?"

Mrs. Logan shook her head. "His plane will probably re-fuel twice during the flight. I'm sure he'll call, if he has the opportunity." She eyed Jamison over the top of her mug. "What about the security plan for the airport tomorrow?"

"Everything's in place, ma'am. We'll have the area well guarded. Only those who have a connection with the bri-gade will be allowed access."

"What time will you get there in the morning?"

He shrugged. "Hard to say. I've got to check on a few things at the airfield tonight, and I'll probably return well before sunrise. Tell the wives they can come as early as they want."

"My guess, Greg Yates will be the first to arrive. He's in charge of the decorating committee. Welcome-home signs need to be hung as soon as possible."

"That won't be a problem. There's a scaffold he can use, and I'll be around to help."

"Chief Wilson called me earlier today." Mrs. Logan sipped her coffee. "He said the families will remain in the terminal and watch the planes touch down on live video."

"That's for your security, ma'am. We don't want any civilians on the tarmac. We'll announce the landing and then program a large clock on the wall to count down the minutes until the unit marches into the secure area."

Michele wrapped her hands around the mug. "Will the general give a welcoming speech?"

Jamison smiled. "He assured me he'll be brief. Your mother will be on the dais with him."

Mrs. Logan laughed. "But I won't be speaking. I agree with the general. The shorter we can keep the formal portion of the ceremony, the better. All the soldiers want is to be reunited with their families."

"You're right about that, ma'am." His gaze turned to Michele. She smiled from across the table, igniting a spark within him.

As if understanding their desire to be alone, Mrs. Logan pushed back her chair. "You two stay put as long as you like, but I need some rest."

Jamison stood as she left the room. Once Mrs. Logan had climbed the stairs, he rounded the table to where Michele sat. Touching her hand, he pulled her to her feet and gently turned her around to face the window.

The curtains were open to the night sky. He pointed to the full moon that shone through the darkness.

"I'm taking that as a good sign," he said, slipping his arms around her waist.

She relaxed against his chest. "You always said moonlight was special."

He dipped his head and rubbed his cheek against hers. "With you in my arms, everything is special."

She turned, her smile warming him. Her blue eyes sparkled like the stars. Michele's lips opened ever so slightly, and suddenly all he could think about was the sweetness of her kisses. Lowering his mouth, he captured hers, and the whole world turned bright for one electrifying minute.

The sensation sent shock waves through his body. For the first time in almost a year, Jamison knew he wasn't a failure. Nothing could stop him with Michele at his side. He would always be the victor because winning Michele was the best prize of all.

He pulled her closer, feeling her feminine softness and inhaling her heady perfume. Wanting to take in every detail of her, he opened his eyes, but instead of Michele he saw the darkness outside and realized, for one terrifying second, everything he thought was good could all be a lie.

The killer was still on the loose and would strike again. Another shoot-out might send Michele running back to Atlanta. If she left him a second time, Jamison didn't know if he could survive.

Michele luxuriated in Jamison's arms, intoxicated with the strength of his embrace and the intensity of his kiss. Being together again proved everything would be all right. Her dad would get home safely. Alice and the military policeman would pull through. She and Jamison would take up where they had left off ten months ago.

With a throaty groan, Jamison pulled away from her and adjusted his tie. Feeling at a loss without his arms around her, Michele turned to follow Jamison's gaze, troubled by his apparent rejection. A military policeman came into view in the yard outside the window.

Jamison hadn't wanted the men guarding the Logan home to see them together. Her initial confusion turned to appreciation for her chivalrous hero. Jamison had a strong sense of propriety and put her honor before his own desire.

"Did he notice us?" she asked.

"We're safe." Jamison's lips twitched in an adorable way that made her want to kiss him again. "It's Stiles, and he's making his rounds. I checked earlier. No one was there when I pulled you close."

She sighed contentedly, enjoying his nearness and the familiar way they had stepped back in time. "If we're going to be on display, perhaps it's time to do the dishes."

Jamison raised his brow teasingly.

She poked him in the ribs. "Consider it payment for your dinner."

"And well worth the meal, but didn't I hear something about cookies?"

She laughed. "I told you I baked for the Hughes children. Leftovers are in the jar by the stove." Pointing him in the right direction, she watched as he slipped off his jacket and hung it over the chair.

He grabbed two cookies and then turned back to her. She laughed again as he shoved one in his mouth and winked good-naturedly as if in appreciation of both her and her baking.

Lost in the moment, Michele thought only of Jamison and the future they could have together. Then she looked down and saw the gun on his hip.

Her levity deflated, knowing the complications that still stood between them. If only Jamison would leave the military and law enforcement and move into another line of work.

"Did you…" She ran water in the sink, grateful for something to focus on instead of his questioning gaze. "Did you always want to be a special agent?"

He let out a breath and dropped the cookie on the counter. His eyes searched hers as if trying to determine the underlying meaning to her question.

"I told you my mother died when I was young and that my dad raised me."

She nodded. "You mentioned he didn't know how to parent."

Jamison shrugged. A wry smile tugged at his lips. "I was sugarcoating the reality of our relationship. My father thought the world owed him everything. If he didn't get what he wanted, he took it."

She turned off the water and reached for a paper towel. "I...I don't understand."

"He was a thief, Michele. We lived on the run, hiding out in fleabag motels, sometimes in whatever car he was able to steal."

"What about the police?"

"They had bigger crimes to handle in most cases. Plus, my dad could sense when the cops were closing in. He'd wake me in the middle of the night so we could hightail out of town."

"How did you attend school?"

"Sometimes he'd take a job, and we'd stay in one place long enough for me to get ahead in my studies. Luckily, learning came easily. When we moved on, he'd tuck my textbooks in the car with me, and I'd work on my own."

Michele felt for the little boy who always had to run away from life. Her own childhood had been filled with stability and love. "But you mentioned throwing the discus in high school."

He nodded. "I needed to complete my senior year in order to get a college scholarship. My dad had a job at the plant in town at that time. The foreman complained he wasn't pulling his fair share of the weight. Dad got mad, picked a fight and came home bloodied and beaten."

Her hand rose to her throat.

"My father was determined to teach the guy a lesson. He had gasoline in the trunk of his car and expected me to go back to the factory with him later that night."

She was afraid to hear what happened.

"I told him I wouldn't do it. We argued." Jamison's face twisted as if he were seeing his father again. "He took off in his car like a madman. I raced after him."

Michele moaned, anticipating the outcome.

"I ran for ten blocks across town to where he worked.

By the time I got there, he had already poured gasoline on lumber that was piled against the corner of the building."

Jamison drew his hand to his chest. "The acrid smell filled my lungs. Dad had a lighter and screamed for me to stay away from him. He said he hated me and who I had become. I tried to reason with him, but he kept saying I was a failure and would never succeed in life."

Michele wished she could wipe away the pain she saw on Jamison's face.

"I stopped in the middle of the street, not knowing whether to rush him and try to pull him away or to just keep talking." He shook his head. "I made the wrong decision that night."

"Oh, Jamison."

"He struck the match. There must have been gasoline on his hands. It had spilled onto his clothes."

Closing the distance between them, Michele wanted to pull him close, but Jamison needed to keep talking.

"I tried to get to him in time." His voice was husky with emotion.

"You did the right thing. You weren't to blame."

Jamison shook his head. "I never wanted to be like him. When I was a kid, he forced me to steal so we could eat. Produce from a farmers' market. Bread from a bakery. Meat from a mom-and-pop grocery store. I knew it was wrong, but I wanted to earn his love."

"You were only a child."

"The army was my way out. Talking to the chaplain, hearing about Jesus's love allowed me to ask forgiveness and put all that behind me. Until ten months ago, when I thought I could talk a gunman down, that he'd listen to reason, just as I thought my father would the night he died in the fire."

Michele remembered all too clearly that deadly day on post.

"I rushed forward to save the shooter because that's what I should have done for my dad. But I made a mistake that almost killed Dawson. I was thinking like a kid, instead of a special agent."

"Oh, Jamison, the reason I left ten months ago was that I couldn't love a man who always put himself in danger. You can leave the military. There are other jobs that don't require you to carry a gun."

He shook his head. "I'm not a guy who runs away like my father did. I have to stay and work through my problems. That's the only way I can live with myself."

She took a step back. "But you said you made a mistake."

He nodded. "That's right."

"Don't you see?" Tears stung her eyes. "I understand what you're going through because I made a mistake that cost my brother his life."

Jamison's face softened and his voice was low when he finally spoke. "The difference between us, Michele, is that I've forgiven myself."

Which was something she could never do.

Frantic to hold on to their fragile relationship, she reached for him. "If you care about me, you'll walk away from the military so we can be together."

His eyes narrowed. "You sound like my father. He put me between his love and what I knew in my heart was right. I won't run away. That's not who I am. The military taught me to be a better man than my father."

Why couldn't Jamison understand? "You can be that better man with me."

He shook his head. "You don't know what you're asking."

A sword pierced her heart, and she gasped at the pain. They were worlds apart. He was the kid who still had to prove himself to his father, and she was the sister who couldn't forgive herself for her brother's death. Neither of them would give up the past to forge a new future together.

A lump formed in her throat. Jamison gazed into her eyes, and she saw that he, too, realized the terrible divide that hung between them, a divide too broad and too deep to cross.

Only she didn't know how she could ever say goodbye to the man she loved. If only something would change his heart.

The phone rang. The shrill tone cut through that divide, bringing them back to the moment, to the reality that one woman had died and two other lives hung in the balance.

Michele reached for the phone. She turned toward the window and glanced outside. The moon had disappeared behind the clouds.

"Colonel Logan's quarters, Michele speaking." She reverted to the greeting she had used growing up when her home was happy and life was good.

"I can see you."

Michele's heart exploded in her chest.

"I'm coming after you, Michele."

The blood drained from her head. She felt light-headed and nauseated.

"You'll be the next to die."

"Michele?" Jamison's voice. Insistent. Demanding. "It's him, isn't it?"

She couldn't respond. All she could do was stare into the darkness where the killer waited.

Jamison followed her gaze. "He's out there."

Drawing his gun, he pulled open the back door and raced into the night.

The killer's maniacal laughter filled the phone. "Before I kill you, I'll kill Steele."

Jamison ran across the backyard. He was that kid, long ago, running to save his father, only tonight he was trying to save her.

"Jamison!" she screamed, racing through the doorway. This time, Dawson and the military police weren't going to take the hit. This time, Jamison would be the one to die.

The night was hot and humid and filled with sounds that intensified the fear hammering at her heart.

"Jamison!" she screamed again.

A bullet whizzed past her, striking the brick wall just a fraction of an inch from her head.

The sound of a second shot cut through the night.

Dazed, she took a step back. Jamison screamed her name. Before she could react, his arms were around her, pulling her to the ground.

A third round exploded.

Jamison gasped. Wet warmth ran down Michele's back. The coppery smell returned, overpowering her.

Without turning to see the blood, Michele knew the terrible truth. Jamison had been hit.

SIXTEEN

"I'm all right," Jamison insisted as the medic finished the triage. The ambulance sat parked in the middle of Michele's backyard surrounded by crime scene experts searching for clues.

Fort Rickman was on lockdown. Military police were canvassing the area, going door to door, and checking every nook and cranny where a man could hide.

"You're one lucky guy," Dawson said, leaning over the stretcher where Jamison lay.

"It's a flesh wound."

"You need stitches."

"The medic bandaged me up, Dawson. I'm fine."

"You're headstrong and not thinking straight. You never should have run into the night."

"Michele told you?"

"She's angry, Jamison, and fed up with you. She's holed up in the house, refusing to see anyone."

"I'll talk to her."

Dawson shook his head. "I wouldn't tonight. Give her time. The medics prescribed a sleeping pill. From what Mrs. Logan said, she hasn't slept the last two nights."

Jamison knew she was exhausted.

"Not that any of us have slept." Dawson stated the obvious. "Look, Jamison, you should have called for backup. McGrunner and Stiles were on the sidewalk in front of the house."

"By the time I contacted them, the killer would have been long gone."

"And you wouldn't have taken a hit."

"It's minor."

"You're one stubborn fool." Dawson's cell rang. He stepped away to take the call.

Mrs. Logan came out of her quarters and walked straight to where Jamison lay.

"How's Michele?" he asked as she neared.

"She's resting. I suggest you wait until tomorrow to talk to her."

"Are you sure, ma'am?"

Mrs. Logan nodded. "Tomorrow will be soon enough."

So much would happen in the morning. Once her father was home, Michele would be free to head back to Atlanta.

"Stanley called," Mrs. Logan continued. "His plane had landed to refuel so he and Michele had a chance to talk. Hearing her father's voice helped. She promised me she'd try to sleep."

Mrs. Logan's gaze was warm as she looked down at Jamison. "You saved her life. I can never thank you enough for being such a hero. If…if you hadn't pushed her to the ground…" She shook her head. "I would have lost my daughter as well as my son."

"I'm not a hero, ma'am."

"Maybe you don't think so, but I do. I'll see you in the morning at the airfield." Turning, she retraced her steps and entered her house.

Dawson neared, smiling. "Good news. We've got him."

Jamison felt a surge of relief. "Who? Where? How?"

"A sergeant, trying to leave post. The front gate security

guards found a gun in his glove compartment. A 9 milli-meter. The bullets in the chamber matched the caliber of slugs we dug out of the brick wall."

"Had the gun been recently fired?"

"Roger that. Plus, he had gunpowder residue on his hands. His name's Kenneth Cramer. Claimed he was out on one of the training ranges doing an impromptu target practice. He's part of the First of the Fifth's rear detach-ment. Seems he wanted to deploy to Afghanistan with the brigade, but he had a medical profile at the time. Guess who made the decision to keep him at Fort Rickman?"

"Major Hughes?"

"Bingo. Now that the unit's coming home, he decided to take his anger out on the major by killing his wife."

Jamison saw a hole in the theory. Namely, why had he come after Alice Rossi? "Is there a connection between Cramer and Sergeant Rossi?"

"We'll find one." Dawson rubbed his hand over his tired face. "It's over, Jamison. We can all breathe a sigh of relief."

"Do me a favor. Keep the guards posted on the Logan home."

"There's no reason, buddy."

"Maybe not, but it would make me feel better."

Dawson shrugged. "Okay. Until morning."

"The chief won't want the information about apprehend-ing the killer to go public until ballistics confirms the bul-lets were fired from Sergeant Cramer's gun."

"Of course. But I'm sure we've got our man."

Jamison wasn't convinced.

Dawson started to walk away, then turned to look back at Jamison. "One more thing. You don't always have to be the hero."

Jamison glanced at the brick quarters. Mrs. Logan had

thanked him for saving Michele, yet he'd been reckless to run from the house into the killer's path.

No matter what Mrs. Logan thought, she was wrong. He hadn't saved Michele. He had placed her in danger. Jamison had been a fool instead of a hero. If he hadn't run from the house, Michele never would have followed him.

"Failure...a disappointment... You'll never succeed, Jamie-boy." The words tumbled through Jamison's mind.

Time was running out. He had to ensure that the plans for the airfield were in place. Dawson might think the killer had been apprehended, but in his gut, Jamison didn't feel it was over yet.

He'd been wrong before, and he had questioned his own ability too many times since Dawson had been wounded. Tonight, he couldn't shake the overwhelming sense that the case wasn't closed. Jamison would wait until the ballistics came back before he'd sigh with relief.

The wound on his side throbbed, but Jamison refused to take the painkiller the medic offered. He didn't want anything to hamper his ability to think clearly. He had a lot to figure out, about the killer, about Michele and what the future would hold.

Right now he needed to finish the job he'd been given. He would protect the women at the airfield and the soldiers coming home from Afghanistan. More than anything, he wanted the homecoming to be a time of joy and not sorrow. Then he thought of Major Hughes and Sergeant Rossi and knew some pain lasted a lifetime.

Michele would go back to Atlanta, and Jamison would ask for a change of assignment. He needed to get away from Fort Rickman and everything that reminded him of Michele. She didn't want him in her life, and he didn't blame her. He had made a terrible mistake. A mistake that had almost cost Michele her life.

* * *

Michele heard the ambulance drive away. The voices in the backyard quieted as, one after another, the military police cars pulled from the curb and headed back to their headquarters.

She stared at the sleeping pill the medic had given her, still on her nightstand. She couldn't and wouldn't take it no matter how much she wanted to sleep. Her father was on a plane coming back to the States. If something happened en route, she wanted to be able to accept the news and deal with it without some type of crutch to take away the pain.

Plus, she needed to be strong for her mother, although tonight—after Jamison had been hit—her mother had been the tower of strength.

Michele had run away from Jamison once more. This time, she had fled into her house instead of all the way to Atlanta. She couldn't face him again. If she did, she'd see the blood and his torn shirt and the bullet that ripped open the flesh on his side.

Once the ambulance had arrived and the medics assured her the wound wasn't life threatening, she had raced into the house overcome with nausea so strong she could hardly hold up her head.

Everything she feared would happen had come true. Jamison had charged into danger, and he'd been wounded. If the killer's aim had been better or if Jamison hadn't pushed her to the floor, he could—*would*—be dead.

The thought brought a sour taste to her mouth as bile bubbled up from her stomach. She rubbed her hands over her abdomen, trying to calm the chaos of fear that swirled within her.

She had tried to warn Jamison, to call him back, to tell him to stay inside with her. He'd ignored her warning and turned his back on caution and common sense. If she needed a sign that she had done the right thing ten months ago, she had one today. The message was as loud as the gunshots that rang through the night.

A door slammed and footsteps signaled her mother was downstairs. Water ran. At this hour, Roberta was probably brewing a cup of herbal tea before she climbed the stairs and went to bed.

A chill slid down Michele's spine. As much as she'd like a warm mug to hold in her hands and hot liquid to temper the frigid cold that washed over her, she couldn't face her mother now.

Roberta liked Jamison. She always had. Without saying as much, Michele knew her mother wondered how her daughter could have left such a good man. Roberta didn't understand Michele's fear that Jamison would walk into danger and be shot, just as had happened tonight.

Her worst nightmare had come true.

She heard a familiar voice outside and stepped toward the window. Pulling back the curtain ever so slightly she saw Jamison and McGrunner deep in conversation.

Farther away, she noticed additional military police patrolling the area around her house. Nothing seemed to have changed, even though she had overheard some of the men talking about the captured killer.

Her mother's footfalls sounded coming up the stairs. She knocked softly on the closed door. "Michele, honey, can I get you anything?"

She stared into the night, unable to answer. Hopefully, her mother would think the pill had worked and she was sound asleep.

McGrunner saluted and walked away. Jamison glanced up at her window. Even at this distance and in the darkness, Michele knew he saw her, and that caused her heart to break.

She loved him more than he would ever know, but she couldn't keep looking over her shoulder wondering when the next gunman would strike. Michele wanted Jamison, but she wanted him alive. She'd rather leave him behind than have her worst fears come true.

SEVENTEEN

Jamison spent most of the night coordinating security between flight personnel at the airfield, the military police and the Criminal Investigation Division. Once everything was in place, he reviewed the operation, checking to ensure that he hadn't missed some seemingly insignificant item that could become a stumbling block during the actual event.

When dealing with the safety of a brigade of soldiers as well as the families who loved them, every detail had to be checked and doubled-checked.

Even though Sergeant Kenneth Cramer was in custody, Jamison didn't have a sense of closure on the case. He used to be able to trust his instincts. Now he was never sure if the signals he was receiving were accurate. Hopefully, with time, his old confidence would return, but the memory of his mistakes still haunted him, especially when lives were at risk.

Corporal Otis arrived at CID headquarters shortly before 0500 hours. He brewed a fresh pot of coffee and poured Jamison the first cup. "Here you go, sir. Strong and black."

Jamison accepted the mug with a nod of gratitude. The

hot brew burned going down, but the effect gave him the burst of energy he needed.

"How are you feeling, sir?" the corporal asked.

"Like I should shower and shave."

"And the wound?"

"A little sore, but not really a problem." In truth, his side ached, although not enough to slow him down.

Otis returned to the main office. Jamison continued to work, not only because of the importance of the mission but also to keep his mind focused on anything except Michele. If he paused for even a moment, images of her from last night tangled through his mind.

He glanced up as Otis reappeared, carrying two donuts and a banana. "I scrounged up breakfast."

Jamison laughed. "You raided someone's stash of snacks."

The corporal laughed. "Sir, I plead the Fifth." He placed the contraband on Jamison's desk. "The chief's secretary told me to help myself anytime I was hungry."

"I'll spring for donuts next week." Jamison took a large bite out of the glazed pastry, enjoying the impromptu meal. After eating, he downed his coffee and stretched back in his chair. "So, tell me, Otis, have you ever been a fool for love?"

His light mocha face twisted into a wide grin. "More times than I'd like to admit."

Tapping a pen against his desk, Jamison hesitated before he asked, "Did you send flowers?"

The soldier nodded his head. "Matter of fact, I use the florist on post any time I want to tell a lady how special she is. Best way I know to get on a woman's good side. Does the trick just like that." He snapped his fingers, which caused Jamison to smile and wonder whether he needed to call the florist this morning and order a bouquet for Michele.

"Little secret I learned at a young age, sir, if you're interested."

Jamison nodded.

"The ladies like roses. Red, yellow, white. The color doesn't matter, but I can attest to the return such an investment might bring on your behalf."

Otis chuckled and headed back to his own desk.

The corporal's wit brought a burst of fresh air into the stuffy office. Feeling encouraged, Jamison closed the files, nodded to Otis as he left the CID headquarters and drove to the gym. Thirty minutes later, Jamison had showered and shaved and donned a fresh white shirt before he headed to the airfield.

His optimism deflated as he drove across post. Flowers wouldn't change the situation with Michele. Jamison had been a fool to get close to her again. Holding her in his arms had wiped away the ten months they had been apart. The pain he felt at the moment was as real and as raw as when she had initially left him.

All his efforts to move forward without her had been foiled last night in her kitchen. He'd told her the moonlight was special, but he'd been wrong. The moon had lulled him into believing he had a chance.

She had seemed so willing to fold into his embrace. Her perfume was hypnotic, her eyes enticing. Touching her was like touching life itself. She was everything to him, but he couldn't walk away from who he was and what he did no matter how much he loved her.

Arriving at the airfield, he quickly ensured that everyone knew their jobs and were ready to execute them flawlessly. Word had spread that the killer was in custody, and a sense of euphoria settled over the military police and CID personnel on duty. Jamison cautioned them not to be lulled into believing the danger had passed. Ballistics needed to confirm the rounds fired at Michele's house matched those from the firearm found in the suspect's vehicle. Until then, Jamison wanted everyone to be vigilant and act as if the killer was still on the loose.

Jamison went person to person, ensuring all the security personnel realized the complexity of keeping the brigade safe and the necessity to be on high alert until the last soldier had left the airfield.

The three planes transporting the soldiers were scheduled to land at approximately 1100 hours. The estimated time of arrival had been released to the Family Readiness Groups, and people had already started to trickle in to the terminal.

Even now a sense of excitement permeated the air. Many groups on post had set up tables to support the families as they waited. The Red Cross provided first-aid stations. The Army Community Services carried in cases of bottled water they chilled on ice and handed out as needed. Morale Support personnel distributed small American flags that children waved as they played near their mothers.

Some of the families dressed alike in T-shirts bearing their hero soldier's picture. Others had buttons that read Proud Army Wife or I love my soldier husband. A few of the women wore stiletto heels and fancy dresses eager to welcome their returning loved ones with more than a kiss.

The army band warmed up their instruments in a corner of the large arena, adding to the growing excitement. Jamison knew the crowd would swell when the doors opened and the men and women in uniform marched into the terminal. He tasked two military policemen to rope off a central area large enough for the unit to stand in formation during the general's welcome.

Following the speeches, the dividers would be dropped, and a huge lovefest would ensue as families and soldiers united. Tears of joy would mix with laughter. Proud parents with beaming faces would embrace their returning sons and daughters. Babies born during the deployment would gaze with blank stares at the soldier dads they had never seen before, while older children squealed with delight and reached for parents who had been out of their lives for too long. Wives would scramble to find their husbands in the throng, and men would open their arms to the person they had dreamed of holding tight for the last twelve months. All of that would play out later today at the homecoming and would be the best part of the celebration.

The worst would be when Major Hughes and Sergeant Rossi were escorted off the plane ahead of the others. Military sedans would be waiting on the tarmac. The chaplain would be part of the transport detail. One van would drive the newly widowed major to the VIP quarters on post, where he would reunite with his children and sister-in-law. Alice's husband would be taken directly to the hospital. Although her condition had improved slightly, the homecoming would be bittersweet for both men.

The news media had requested to be on-site to film the welcome-home ceremony. Returning soldiers sold airtime, and the TV stations wanted to capture the event for the nightly news. Owing to the need for security, Jamison had recommended they remain off post. Chief Agent in Charge Wilson and the commanding general had agreed with his assessment.

The sound of raised voices came from a side entrance to the terminal. Jamison hustled toward the commotion. A vendor wearing a shirt with the Freemont Sandwich Shoppe logo was growing increasingly antagonistic toward an MP guarding the door.

"Look, I've got cases of sandwiches we plan to sell today," the bulky civilian complained. "Why do all of them have to be searched?"

The MP stood his ground. "Sir, we need to check everything that passes through these doors."

"Is there a problem?" Jamison asked as he approached, flashing his identification. He glanced at the vendor's name tag. Rick Stallings.

Jamison's presence had a calming effect, but the vendor continued to state his case. "Here's the thing, sir. I've got cases of sandwiches we've been authorized to sell today. They're wrapped and crated." Stallings pointed to the MP. "This guy tells me he needs to check everything.

"Every case," the MP explained. "Not every sandwich. If you'll give us a little cooperation, we'll have you through the checkpoint so you can set up your concession table."

The vendor hesitated, then sighed. His body language shifted from confrontation to acceptance.

Still concerned by the outburst, Jamison took the guard aside. "Do a thorough search of Mr. Stallings and his merchandise."

"I'll take care of it, sir."

Pulling the complainer out of line, a guard frisked him, while two other military policemen checked the cases of sandwiches. When the search was completed, the ranking MP nodded to Jamison. "He's good to go, sir."

Stepping away from the security checkpoint, Jamison raised the handheld radio that connected him to the security detail. He cautioned law enforcement to keep their eyes on the people working in the concession area as well as the family members.

Once Stallings had moved on, one of the guards sidled over to Jamison. "That guy's a problem waiting to happen, sir. Makes me grateful for the ones who cooperate."

He pointed over his shoulder. "The florist was the complete opposite. He insisted I check him out when he arrived with his flowers."

Jamison turned to see Teddy Sutherland surrounded by a number of plastic buckets that held long-stem yellow roses.

"Had to cost him a pretty penny, sir, for all those flowers," the guard continued. "He wanted to do something special. Said he owed Colonel Logan. That's the type of guy who understands the military."

As much as Michele loved flowers, Jamison hoped Teddy would have a few roses left over, in case she showed signs of changing her mind. A bouquet of flowers might help to soften her heart toward Jamison and the military.

A number of wives he had seen at Mrs. Logan's quarters and at the brigade barracks yesterday arrived with homemade posters in hand, all welcoming the soldiers back to Fort Rickman.

Greg Yates followed them through security, carting a large oilcloth sign, professionally designed. Jamison had the scaffolding positioned so the tarp could be hung near the giant wall clock, as the military spouse requested.

"Do you need some help?" he yelled up to Yates, who seemed to be having trouble attaching the last corner of the sign.

The guy climbed down and shook his head. "For the life of me, I can't seem to get the grommet over the hook. It's probably fatigue. I drove my son to the airport last night." He tugged at the collar of his shirt with frustration. Noting his shaking hand, Jamison raised his brow. "Is anything else bothering you?"

Yates shrugged. "I haven't seen my wife since R & R. That was five and a half months ago. A lot can happen in that length of time."

Jamison knew how relationships could change.

"How 'bout I give you a hand?" Jamison took off his jacket and handed it to Yates, who scurried to the nearby concession area and tossed the sports coat over the back of a folding chair.

Jamison knew he had made a mistake when he climbed to the top of the scaffold. Not only did his side ache, but he felt moisture seep from under the bandage. Hopefully, not blood.

Grabbing the edge of the sign, he adjusted the hook and the grommet fell into place. He called down to Yates, "How's it look?"

"A little higher."

Jamison adjusted the tarp and waited for Yates's approval. A wide smile and a thumbs-up confirmed the sign was in place.

Climbing down, Jamison spied Rick Stallings sitting in one of the folding chairs next to his sports coat. The guy had a sandwich wrapper on his lap and was shoving what looked like a ham and cheese on rye into his mouth. Just so he didn't spray mustard.

By the time Jamison retrieved his jacket, Stallings had returned to the concession area and was hard at work.

The florist stood near the front door, handing flowers to the ladies who entered. The expressions on their faces confirmed their appreciation. Teddy seemed almost jovial. The somber mood that had gripped the post had lifted now that the brigade was coming home.

Jamison glanced at his watch. It was only 6:45 a.m., but a crowd was starting to form already. Everyone wanted to stake out an area close to the center of the terminal in order to have a good view when the unit marched forward. Being with other families enhanced the excitement as they waited for the planes to land.

He radioed the timekeeper in charge of the clock. "Do we have a definite arrival time for the brigade?"

"Yes, sir. Eleven-oh-five."

"Let's begin the countdown at eight hundred hours."

"Roger that, sir."

Lowering the radio, Jamison surveyed the terminal. Nothing should go wrong, but he knew that anything could happen. Like last night when he'd had his arms around Michele and had started to imagine what the future could hold. Just that fast, everything had changed.

He glanced once again at the giant clock. Mrs. Logan was scheduled to arrive between nine and ten o'clock. Michele would probably arrive with her. Hopefully, he'd have time to talk to her before the planes landed. As much as he longed to spend the rest of his life with Michele, he couldn't compromise who he was. If she needed to change him, then she had never loved him in the first place.

No matter how much he hoped it wasn't true, Michele would probably leave Fort Rickman and return to Atlanta. He would try to carry on as best he could, but the thought of living life without Michele left a hole in his heart, a hole he doubted he would ever be able to fill.

Michele woke at 7:00 a.m., feeling like bread dough that had been kneaded too long. The muscle in her back still ached, and the bruise on her thigh looked like green marble with a swirl of yellow.

She glanced at the sleeping pill still on her dresser. As much as she had wanted to rest, she was glad she had skipped the medication. Padding downstairs, she perked coffee and took a steaming mug upstairs while she changed into navy slacks and a red, white and blue silk top. She attached an American flag pin to her collar.

The Cross My Heart necklace lay on her dresser near

the Bible she had pulled out of her drawer last night. When sleep had eluded her, she'd found comfort in the familiar scripture passages she had loved in her youth.

Michele reached for the necklace, not because of the heart charm Jamison had given her, but because of the cross that had been a gift from Lance. Her father's plane would land in a few hours, and their small family would be together again. Wanting something that represented her brother, she hooked the chain around her neck.

Before heading downstairs, Michele peered into her parents' bedroom. "Can I bring you some coffee?" she asked her mother.

"Not now, dear. I woke up with a headache and want to stay in bed a bit longer."

Probably because of the stress Roberta had been under.

Downstairs, Michele entered the kitchen, thinking of last night and everything Jamison had told her about his childhood. The story of his past had been painful to recount. No doubt, living that life had been even more difficult.

Wrapping her arms around her waist, Michele stared out the window. Sunshine streamed into the kitchen and held the promise of what the new day would bring.

More than anything, she wanted to hold Jamison and feel his arms around her. If the gap between them wasn't so large, there might be hope for them. Then she sighed, realizing she was being foolish. Hope had disappeared last night.

A knock sounded on the front door. Peering through the window, she saw McGrunner standing on the front steps.

Opening the door, she smiled. "Morning, Corporal."

"Ma'am." He glanced down at the cell phone in his hand. "I received a text message from Special Agent Steele. He wants you to meet him at the airfield as soon as possible to discuss how the day's events will unfold. He mentioned needing help arranging some of the banners and flags."

"I thought a committee was decorating the terminal."

McGrunner shrugged. "All I know, ma'am, is that Agent Steele said he didn't want to disrupt your mother this early."

"Are you supposed to follow me to the airfield?"

"No, ma'am. A suspect's in custody, and Agent Timmons pulled the guard detail from your quarters as of this morning. Agent Steele directed me to escort your mother to the airfield, and I plan to do what he requested."

"Yes, of course." Already, she missed Jamison's protective closeness.

McGrunner glanced once again at the phone in his hand. "Agent Steele said traffic might be backed up on post with everyone heading to physical training. He suggested you take the back road that weaves through the training area. No one will be using that route at this time of the morning, and you won't be hung up with any delays."

Mrs. Logan was sleeping by the time Michele went back upstairs. Not wanting to disturb her mother's slumber, Michele wrote a note and explained the reason she had gone ahead to the airfield.

Waving to McGrunner as she left the quarters, Michele slipped behind the wheel of her car and headed toward the training area. After making a number of turns, she realized Jamison had been right. No one was on the road in that remote part of the post.

The weather report on the radio called for clear skies and sunshine, a welcome relief after the storms and overcast skies. Her father would be home within a few hours, and she wouldn't have to worry about his safety any longer.

Plus, Jamison had asked to see her, which she took as a good sign. Maybe he had changed his mind about the military or was ready to make a compromise that could keep them together. A surge of elation she hadn't expected flowed through her. Knowing she would see him soon opened a door deep within her, a door she had thought would never open again.

Up ahead, the narrow road curved to the right. She eased up on the accelerator. Halfway through the curve, she jammed on the brakes. Her car screeched to a stop, almost hitting a beige van stalled across the roadway. The side panel on the truck read Prime Maintenance.

An accident? A deer could have run in front of the van. She pulled her cell phone from her purse to call the military police, then decided to see if anyone was hurt first. Michele opened the door and stepped onto the pavement.

She approached the vehicle and put her hands against the driver's window to peer inside. The front seat was vacant. Michele tried to see into the rear of the truck, then startled as a twig snapped behind her.

A warning flashed through her mind.

Footsteps sounded on the pavement.

She pivoted and raised her hand protectively as a man wearing a ski mask jammed a stun gun against her arm.

Pain ricocheted through her body. Her muscles convulsed. Unable to maintain her balance, she fell to the pavement. Her forehead cracked against the asphalt.

Inwardly, she screamed, yet only a guttural groan issued from her mouth. Fear clamped down on her spastic spine.

All she could see were the military boots of the man standing over her. His laughter mixed with her panic and caused her heart to pound at breakneck speed. Even if she survived her body's contortions, she would never survive him.

"I've got you now, Michele," he said with a sneer. "You're going to die."

EIGHTEEN

Michele moaned. Lulled by the motion of the moving vehicle, she longed to remain in the semiunconscious darkness. If she opened her eyes, the terror of what had happened would be real.

Her head throbbed, and her muscles screamed in protest. She lay next to the side of the van with her cheek pressed against the metal flooring, and her hands tied behind her back. She tried to turn over, but her feet were bound, as well.

A blanket covered her, and although the van was air-conditioned, sweat dampened her neck and under her arms. The stale smell of the thick wool sickened her. A wide strip of tape covered her mouth. If she got sick, she would gag on her own bile. Asphyxiation wasn't the way she wanted to die.

Michele thought of Jamison and longed for the strength of his arms and the protection only he could provide. She had run away from him last night after telling him she didn't want him in her life.

Another mistake.

She had made too many.

Michele had lost Jamison. She was about to lose something else today.

Her life.

* * *

Mrs. Logan arrived at the terminal shortly after 9:00 a.m., dressed in a navy suit with white blouse and a patriotic-print scarf tied around her neck. From where Jamison stood at the far end of the terminal, he was struck by how much Michele resembled her mother with her big eyes and high cheekbones.

To her credit, Mrs. Logan still had a youthful vitality. Confident Michele would be beautiful at each stage of life, Jamison wanted to be the man at her side, but he feared that dream would never come true. Not after last night.

Always the dedicated First Lady of the brigade, Mrs. Logan talked to the wives and children who gathered close to the security rope. Everyone carried cameras and signs and American flags they had received as they entered the terminal. A number of the wives held the yellow roses Teddy had distributed.

The clock on the wall ticked off the time.

Seeing Jamison, Mrs. Logan waved and walked toward him.

He met her halfway. "Morning, ma'am. Everything's ready."

She looked around the terminal and smiled. "You've done an excellent job, Jamison."

"A lot of folks wanted to get involved." He glanced at the concession area. "As you can see, we've got food and drinks for the families as they wait. A magician will entertain the children at 0945. Once his act is over, we'll show cartoons on the giant wall screen until the planes fly into Georgia airspace. At that point, we'll broadcast a map pinpointing the flight progress."

"And the families will be able to watch the planes land?"

"Yes, ma'am. Via a live video feed that will stream onto the big screen."

"Wonderful." Once again, she glanced around the terminal, but when she looked back at him, her brow was creased. "Have you seen Michele?"

"As far as I know, she hasn't arrived yet."

"That's impossible." Mrs. Logan's hand touched her collar. "She left the house some time ago."

A drum pounded in Jamison's temple. "Could she have gone back to Atlanta?"

"Absolutely not. Michele wanted to be here when Stanley's plane landed. She left me a note saying she was driving to the terminal to meet you. Corporal McGrunner said you had contacted him about needing Michele's help."

Jamison's heart thumped a warning as he called the corporal on his cell. "Where are you?"

"Directly outside the terminal, sir."

"You told Mrs. Logan I called you this morning?"

"Not a phone call, sir. You sent a text message."

Jamison hit the text icon on his phone. Filled with dread, he read the message he was supposed to have written. Someone had accessed the cell phone he kept in his coat pocket.

Greg Yates had taken his jacket when Jamison was on the scaffold. Turning his gaze to the concession area, he searched for Rick Stallings, who had eaten a sandwich seated right next to Jamison's jacket when he was adjusting the tarp. Would either man have been able to retrieve the cell and send the text?

Mrs. Logan grabbed his hand. "What's happened, Jamison?"

Before he could answer, his cell phone rang. He glanced at Dawson's name highlighted on the caller ID.

"We've got a huge problem," Jamison said as he raised the cell to his ear.

"You can say that again, buddy. Ballistics called. The

initial exam of the bullets shows a disparity in the markings. Although nothing is definite yet, it looks like Sergeant Kenneth Cramer may have been telling the truth."

Jamison's heart jammed in his throat as more pieces of the puzzle fell into place. The killer was on the loose, and he had Michele.

NINETEEN

Michele woke with a start. For an instant, she forgot about the killer and his van and the smelly blanket that covered her.

Then her memory returned full force. Tears stung her eyes, but she couldn't cry. She had to remain alert and ready for any opportunity to get away from him, whoever he was. All she knew was that he had killed before, and he would kill again.

The sound of his voice filled the van and made her skin crawl. He was ranting about her father, Major Hughes and Sergeant Rossi. She couldn't make out everything he said over the hum of the van's motor, but she heard enough to know he was delusional. As she listened, she began to understand why he had killed Yolanda and tried to end Alice Rossi's life as well as her own.

Michele tugged at the restraints on her hands and legs until her flesh was raw. She tried to roll over, hoping to free herself from the blanket. Her leg struck against something that toppled onto the floor of the van. The crash of metal upon metal made her heart pound even harder.

He stopped his tirade.

Michele lay still, barely breathing. If not for the blanket, she would be able to see what he was doing and read the expression on his face. As it was, she was surrounded by darkness.

The van slowed. He pulled off the road and braked to a stop. Waves of nausea rolled over her. She needed to be strong, but she wasn't. She was scared to death.

Her heart raced, and her pulse pounded in her ear.

The driver's door opened and then slammed, sending a volley of aftershocks exploding through her head. Footfalls sounded on the pavement as he rounded the van.

She tried to scream, but the duct tape muffled her cries for help. Her throat burned, and her mouth was as dry as sandpaper. She jerked her head from side to side, struggling against the putrid blanket.

Oh, God, help me!

If he opened the rear doors, she might be able to kick him or hurl herself onto the roadway. Surely someone driving by would see her. Then she listened and heard nothing except his footsteps and her pounding heart.

A rear door opened. He grabbed her ankles and yanked her along the rough metal bed of the van that scraped her cheek. She thrashed her feet, needing to free her legs from his hold.

He continued to spit hateful words about her father and his former battalion and how everyone would pay. He talked about cutting into Lance's gravestone and other things that didn't make sense, but nothing made sense about a man who killed.

Then he laughed. The sound sent another round of shock waves through her body. She tried to backpedal. His fingers gripped her upper arm. Michele expected to crash onto the pavement at any second.

What she hadn't expected was the stun gun. The violent shock caused her back to arch. Repeated spasms racked her muscles. Her legs and arms writhed and convulsed and twisted in tandem as the restraints held. Pain radiated throughout her body and sapped the little strength she had left.

Her head exploded. She saw bursts of white lightning and then, when she couldn't endure anything more, she slipped away into darkness.

Jamison jammed his cell phone closer to his ear. "I'm leaving the terminal to search for Michele," he told Dawson after filling him in on the text message.

"Stay where you are until I get to the airport. I'm headed there now."

Disconnecting, Jamison pocketed his phone, feeling as if he'd been beaten to a pulp with a steel beam. Just as in his youth, everything was spiraling out of control, and he couldn't react fast enough, or think decisively enough or have the vision he needed to get into the killer's point of view. Where was Michele?

As a CID agent who had handled numerous investigations, Jamison knew what could happen, what might already have happened. The realization sent waves of terror through him that chilled him to the core.

His eyes turned to where Rick Stallings was working at the concession stand. Not far away, Greg Yates sipped coffee and glanced at the giant clock on the wall.

Jamison barked a number of orders into the security radio. Responding immediately, four military guards removed the two men, without incident, from the central area of the terminal and sequestered each of them in separate office rooms located toward the rear of the large complex.

Although Jamison needed to question the men, he had to inform Mrs. Logan about the current situation. When he turned to face her, he realized she was well aware of what had happened. Her eyes reflected his own fears, sending another jab of pain deep to his gut.

Looking suddenly older than her years, she took his hand and held it tight. "You'll find her, Jamison. You have to."

He wished he shared her confidence. "Yes, ma'am."

She shook her head, perhaps sensing his own faltering optimism. "I don't want the wives to know what has happened. The spouses and family members have worried enough and need this time to welcome their husbands home."

He had to object. "Ma'am, our first priority is to find Michele."

"That's what I want, as well, Jamison. But the brigade needs a homecoming. Nothing should be canceled unless it specifically impacts my daughter's safety."

At some point, Mrs. Logan needed to put her family's well-being before the brigade's. "Ma'am, there's a lounge located near the Red Cross first-aid station, if you'd like someplace to wait."

He radioed one of the female soldiers in the military police detail to escort the colonel's wife to the lounge and remain with her at all times.

Jamison admired Mrs. Logan's grit, but he didn't want his hands tied when it came to finding Michele. If he had to halt the welcome-home celebration, he would. He would do anything to save Michele.

But right now he needed to move forward. Fast.

Hastening toward the rear of the terminal, he entered the first office.

"Where is she?" Jamison demanded, leaning across the conference table where Stallings sat. Given any sign of provocation, Jamison would throw him against the wall and pound the truth out of him.

The vendor's eyes widened, antagonism evident as he bristled. "What are you talking about?"

"I'm talking about a missing woman. And that's on top of one woman murdered, another in critical condition and a military policeman who may have to get a medical discharge because of you."

"You've got the wrong guy."

"Where were you this morning?"

"At the sandwich shop in Freemont. You can call my boss. We worked most of the night, preparing the food for today."

"What time did you arrive on post?"

"Uh—" Stallings hesitated.

"Trying to do the math and make it all work out in your favor? Your information was captured electronically when you showed your identification to the guard at the Main Gate. Won't take long to retrieve the time."

"Traffic was backed up getting on post. I'm not sure when I actually passed through security."

Jamison changed gears. "Do you like to text?"

Surprised by the question, Stallings pushed back in his chair. Jamison leaned in closer, knowing he was emotional and apt to do something he would later regret, but he needed information.

The door to the office opened. Corporal Otis motioned to Jamison. "Sir."

"What?" Jamison demanded in the hallway, his anger on a short fuse.

"Special Agent Warner, from Afghanistan, called CID headquarters asking to speak to you, sir. He said it involved our case."

Jamison glanced at the nearby office where Greg Yates waited. Maybe everything was about to break.

Punching Speed Dial on his cell, Jamison was relieved

when Warner answered. "Major Shirley Yates appears to be squeaky clean. No involvements on this side of the world."

"There were rumors of infidelity."

"Rumors that got out of hand."

"Are you sure there wasn't some truth behind them?"

"Not that we could uncover. She was mentoring a captain, prior enlisted. The guy had run into a little problem with his report of survey. He had signed for equipment that he couldn't account for when the brigade was getting ready to redeploy home. The captain was about her age. They spent time together and tongues wagged. You know how that is. Everyone jumps to the wrong conclusion."

Which was exactly what Jamison had done concerning the major's husband. Glancing at the room where Rick Stallings waited, he realized he might have been wrong about both men.

Jamison blew out a lungful of air. Right now all he wanted to do was pound his fist into the wall until it was bloodied. Somehow he needed to feel the pain he feared Michele was experiencing. "Please, God, no."

"Jamison?"

He turned to find Dawson approaching him from the central terminal. "I've got military police canvassing the colonel's housing area. Fort Rickman's under lockdown. The only people who are being allowed on post are active duty personnel and then only after a thorough search of their vehicles and person."

"I'm more concerned about anyone leaving the garrison."

"No one's allowed off at this point."

"What about the training area?"

"The military police have been along the back roads

from the Logan home to the airfield. No one has spotted her yet. Now they're searching the ranges, one at a time."

Which would take hours.

Jamison quickly filled Dawson in on Stallings and Yates. "I can't stay, Dawson. I've got to find Michele."

As he raced out of the terminal, Jamison looked up at the bright sky. "God, I need your help today, more than I've ever needed anything."

He couldn't rely on his own ability. He had made too many mistakes. He had to rely on the Lord so that this time his mistakes didn't end in tragedy. If Jamison lost Michele, he lost everything, maybe even his soul.

TWENTY

Michele knew she was alone because of the silence. No running motor, no air-conditioning, no jumbled ramblings from a delusional killer. All she heard was her heart pounding. Then voices in the distance.

If only she could attract someone's attention. She raised her legs and kicked the wall of the van over and over again, until her muscles ached, and her energy was sapped.

The blanket, wrapped around her face, constricted her breathing. In the closed vehicle and with the hot August day, the temperature had risen too fast. Frantic, Michele fought against the thick wool blanket around her face and felt instant elation when a portion of the covering slipped aside. Like a crazed woman, she inhaled the stale, hot air.

Sweat beaded on her upper lip and dampened her neck. The temperature rose even higher. How long could a person survive in an enclosed vehicle? She didn't want an answer and wished she hadn't even thought of the question.

If You're a loving God, I'm begging You to help me. I've made so many mistakes. Forgive me, Father.

Michele had been wrong about Jamison. He was a wonderful man, and she wasn't worthy of his love. If only she could tell him, but it was too late.

If Alice didn't pull through, three women would have

died because of a maniac who wanted revenge. God had nothing to do with him and everything to do with Jamison and the other good people in law enforcement who put their lives on the line to help others.

Instead of running away from Jamison, Michele should have been running into his arms.

Jamison drove like a madman, backtracking through the training area along the deserted road Michele must have traveled earlier. He had to find her.

Flicking his gaze right and then left, he hoped to catch sight of her, of her car, of something the military police had missed that would provide a clue to her disappearance. The only thing he knew was the killer had taken her. But where?

Jamison wouldn't allow his mind to imagine what had been done to her. *Please, God, keep Michele safe.*

He shouldn't have left her alone last night. He should have checked on her this morning. He wished he had told her he loved her and needed her and would do anything to be with her.

Right now the thought of a quiet civilian existence sounded perfect, a life where Michele would be safe. If anything happened to her, he'd never be able to forgive himself.

He was a trained special agent. How could he have let a killer get to Michele?

"You're a failure. You'll never succeed."

His father's words played over in his mind. But his dad's wasn't the only voice he heard. Jamison was berating himself, as well.

"Think! Think!" he screamed to no one except the tall Georgia pine trees that edged the training area. "Where could she be?"

The road curved up ahead. Jamison lifted his foot from the accelerator. Before he completed the curve, sunlight reflected off something in the woods. He stomped on the brake.

Leaping from his car, he raced across the narrow asphalt roadway and pressed through the dense wooded area that opened into a clearing where he found Michele's car. The ground was still damp from the storms two nights ago, and thick, red Georgia clay caked her tires.

He searched the area, looking for signs of a struggle. The only thing he found was a muddy boot print.

Jamison fisted his hands with rage. The killer had ambushed her. Maybe he had flagged her down, pretending to be hurt. Then he'd tried to hide her car in the woods, but the wheels had stuck in the mud.

He called Dawson. "I found Michele's vehicle hidden in the woods just east of the live-fire training range. I want it gone over from top to bottom. We need fingerprints that can lead us to the killer. There's a boot print located approximately five feet from the hood of the car, size 11 or 12."

"I'll send a team to check out the vehicle. Right now I'm headed out to the tarmac. The brigade's due to land ahead of schedule." Dawson paused for a long moment. "Look, buddy, I'm to blame on this one, and I owe you an apology."

"For what?"

"For being so confident Sergeant Cramer was the killer. You told me to wait until the ballistics report came back. I was too pigheaded to listen. You were right last night. You were also right ten months ago."

"What are you talking about, Dawson? I was the one who suggested we confront the shooter."

"After I insisted we close in. You wanted to wait until backup was in place."

"You've got it wrong."

"No way, Jamison. I've relived what happened a million times. I got us into it at the beginning."

"The chief's well aware of who was at fault."

"That's why he assigned you to handle the security at the airfield. He knew we'd all work together to track down the killer. He wanted his best and brightest to ensure the safety of the entire brigade."

Jamison didn't have time to process what Dawson had told him. He needed to keep looking for Michele.

Disconnecting, Jamison turned back to his car. Glancing down, he spied something he had missed earlier.

Michele's Cross My Heart necklace. The clasp had broken, and the necklace must have fallen to the ground. He had visions of the killer roughhousing her. The images sent ice-cold terror through his veins.

"Please, God." He reached for the necklace. "I've got to find Michele."

His cell rang. "This is Steele."

Dawson's voice. "The chief wants you back at the terminal. Now."

"I need to keep searching."

"He wants to make sure the homecoming goes off without a glitch."

Jamison knew the real reason. Chief Wilson didn't want a special agent who was emotionally involved with the case to do something that would reflect badly on the CID.

"You're a failure...a disappointment."

Jamison wanted to ignore the chief. Michele was more important than any order from a superior.

Before he gave breath to the words, Jamison saw something else on the pavement. Something that didn't make sense in the middle of the training area.

Stooping, he picked it up and examined it in the sunlight. A long shot, one he didn't want to discuss with Dawson. Only one way to find out if it would lead him to Michele.

"Tell Chief Wilson I'm heading back to the terminal."

TWENTY-ONE

Jamison raced into the terminal, grabbed the military guards at the doors and ordered them to sweep the area. As they took off in opposite directions, he circled through the swarm of people, needing to connect what he had found on the back road with someone here in the building.

The band stood ready in the far corner. Video played over the large overhead screen. The live feed showed the soldiers disembarking from the three planes parked on the tarmac. Cheers erupted when families recognized their loved ones. The excitement was palpable and then grew even more so as the soldiers made their way toward the terminal.

On the opposite side of the arena, one person stood out from the crowd. Jamison raised the radio and gave specific orders to the security patrols.

The guy pushed through the throng and headed for a rear door. Seeing families reunited would be too painful for a prior military guy who felt as if he had "died" when he was redeployed home.

Jamison raced forward, shouting more orders into the radio. His gut tightened as he realized the back door wasn't being guarded. "Rear door security, return to your position. Return to your position."

Following him outside, Jamison spied the van at the edge of the overflow parking area, away from any other vehicles. The guy had opened the driver's door and was climbing inside.

Expecting to hear the sound of backup behind him, Jamison looked down at the radio. He groaned inwardly seeing the flashing red light. Low battery. He tossed the useless device and didn't have time to pull out his cell.

"Wait up," Jamison called, hand on his hip as he neared the van.

The guy had slipped behind the wheel and closed the driver's door. He smiled through the open window as if he didn't have a care in the world. "How's it goin', sir?"

"You tell me."

"No problem, except I've got a delivery to make across post."

"A delivery of flowers for some lucky army wife, waiting for her husband to return home?"

Teddy Sutherland dropped the smile and raised the 9 mm Beretta he held in his hand.

Before Jamison could draw his own weapon, a round exploded into his left shoulder, throwing him back against the van. He grabbed for the sign on the side of the delivery truck to keep his balance. The metal strip bearing the floral logo ripped free and dropped to the pavement, exposing another interchangeable magnetic sign underneath: Prime Maintenance.

Once again, Teddy leaned out the window and took another shot at Jamison. The second round missed him by a breath.

The engine roared to life. The van lurched forward. Jamison pulled open the door and grabbed the florist. The wheel turned, and the van rammed into the light pole that twisted on impact.

Jamison yanked him to the asphalt and pulled his own weapon. "Where is she? Where's Michele?"

"You'll never find her."

Jamison wanted to crash his fist into the sneer covering the florist's twisted face.

Footsteps pounded pavement. McGrunner came running.

"Cuff him," Jamison ordered. "And call Dawson. Tell him we've got the killer."

Jamison raced to the rear of the van. He pulled open the door and shoved aside cardboard cartons containing roses that had wilted in the heat. The smell of decaying flowers hung in the hot air.

A wool army blanket. He lifted the corner.

Relief swept over him.

Michele.

But when he looked closer, he saw her flushed face and her labored breathing.

He'd found her—but was he too late?

Michele jerked as the tape was ripped from her mouth. She blinked her eyes open and saw Jamison.

Screaming for water, he cut through the ropes that bound her hands and legs. "You're going to be okay, honey."

She reached for him. "Oh…Ja…Jamison."

He grabbed the water bottle McGrunner shoved into his hand and held it up to Michele's lips. She drank gratefully. Wetting his handkerchief, he wiped her face with the cooling cloth.

"Teddy—" She had to tell Jamison everything the florist had said as he drove along the back roads. "He…he kept talking about my dad and what happened in the past.

Teddy worked for Yolanda's and Alice's husbands when my father had his battalion."

"In Iraq?" Jamison asked.

Michele nodded. "He…he asked to come home early. His wife…was running around."

"They refused his request." Jamison filled in the blanks.

"My…my father did, as well. Teddy's wife ran off with the boyfriend. No one was there to meet him when the unit redeployed home. Then he—" Michele choked on the words. "He found her and killed her."

"And came back to Fort Rickman. But why did he open a floral shop?"

"The store had been his wife's dream."

Jamison nodded as if he could see how it all unfolded. "Once he found both men were serving in the same brigade, he decided to kill their wives."

"And my mother. Then I got in the way."

She shook her head. "He…he said, when the men marched into the terminal, everyone would suffer. He called it a patriotic homecoming…like…like fireworks on the Fourth of July."

"'Fireworks'? That was the word he used?"

She nodded, but Jamison was already out of the van. "McGrunner will take care of you," he yelled, looking back one last time.

She reached for him, but Jamison was running toward the terminal. Running into danger, just as he'd done last night.

"Oh, God," Michele cried. "Don't let him die."

TWENTY-TWO

The band played a patriotic march. Throngs of people swelled forward toward the cordoned off area. Cameras were poised to take pictures of the soldiers that would soon march into the terminal.

Seconds ticked off the giant clock.

Not enough time.

"We've got a bomb!" Jamison screamed into the radio he had grabbed from McGrunner as he ran into the terminal. "Clear the area. Stop the brigade."

"Sir, you're breaking up," the message came back. "Repeat all after—"

Static. Squelch.

Jamison shouted the orders again and again.

The large clock on the wall continued its countdown.

Ten…nine…eight…

His heart pounded. His throat went dry.

"Fan through the crowd." He motioned to the military police gathered around him. "Herd the people out of the building."

The giant double doors opened.

The brigade stood in formation ready to march forward on command. A sea of American flags fluttered. Screams of joy erupted from the crowd around him.

Jamison's gaze turned to the dais.

The general stood at the microphone. Mrs. Logan was next to him. Her eyes were on Jamison, begging for information.

He nodded, and the relief on her face told him she understood her daughter was safe. What she didn't know was that she and everyone else in the terminal were in danger.

Jamison had to find the bomb before it detonated, before the terminal exploded, before more people died.

Glancing down, he spied something under the platform where Mrs. Logan and the general stood. Something the same color as the flower petal he had found on the pavement in the training area.

All around him throngs of people strained to see their returning loved ones. *Please, Lord.*

He pushed through the crowd, weaving his way forward, surrounded by the groundswell of excitement and the thump of the band's rousing military march pounding in his ears.

Seven…six…

Nearing the platform, he focused on the bucket containing yellow roses. His fingers closed around the handle. He pulled the container forward and peered down into the water, seeing a bundle of wires wrapped in plastic and taped to the bottom of the container.

Five…

The wall clock counted down the seconds.

Bucket in hand, he raced toward the side exit behind the dais.

Four…

Needing to clear the building, he willed his legs to move faster.

Three…

He pushed on the door. Drums pounded out a cadence.

The cheering reached a fever pitch as the soldiers began to march into the central area.

No time.

The tarmac lay before him.

Two…

Pulling in an even breath, he started to wind like a coiled spring, just as he had done throwing the discus in high school. Shoulders balanced. Weight even. He circled, building momentum.

One…

Release.

The bucket left his hand.

The band played. Men marched. The crowd cheered.

The bomb flew through the air and exploded over the tarmac.

Jamison gasped for air and clutched his side. He turned, needing to go back inside, not sure he could find the strength.

"Oh, Jamison." Michele's voice. She wasn't running away, she was running toward him.

"You saved my life. You saved everyone's life. I…I…"

He held up his hand to stop her. The last thing he needed was false hope.

"It's my job, Michele. It's what I do. I love you more than anything, more than life itself, but I have to be true to who I am. That's the only way I can look myself in the eye each day. I've got to make a contribution in this life, and I'm making a difference in the military."

She stopped, her arms still outstretched. She had been through so much today. Her face was scraped and smudged with dirt, but the look he saw in her eyes filled him with encouragement.

"Oh, Jamison, I was thinking only of my own needs before and not what we could be together. You built your life on a firm foundation of God and military and knew what was right and what was wrong. It took me longer to find out what's important. 'God first' is what Lance always told me. I understand that now. God first and the man I love second. I know it's the same for you—that you need to follow God's path for your life, regardless of whether or not I approve."

She stepped closer, her arms inviting him. "The man I love is you, Jamison. I want to keep on loving you forever."

He stepped into her sweet embrace.

Those in the terminal were oblivious to what had happened as cheers of joy and patriotic strains from the band mixed with the revelry of the soldiers who had been gone so long and were once again in the arms of their loved ones.

On the tarmac, Jamison lowered his lips to Michele's, knowing the negative voice from his past had been silenced. He was a new man, a better man, a triumphant man because, in spite of all the mistakes he had made in life, Michele had come back to him.

"Welcome home," he whispered as he kissed her again and again and again.

EPILOGUE

Michele was giddy with excitement.

"What time is Jamison picking you up, dear?" her mother called from the kitchen.

"Six-fifteen."

Her father came down the steps, looking a bit more rested after two weeks of block leave. He had lost weight in Afghanistan and his hair had grayed, but his smile was as wide as ever and his eyes were beginning to twinkle again. The war and the stress of command had taken its toll on him, just as his deployment had been hard on the family he had left behind.

Stepping into the hallway, Roberta stared up at her husband and smiled. "Did you have a good nap, dear?"

"You're making me feel like an old man, Roberta."

She laughed playfully, and Michele realized there was nothing old about either of them or the love they had for each other.

"Erica Grayson called," Roberta informed him. "Curtis, Yolanda's sister and the children are having dinner with the Graysons tonight. Spur-of-the-moment, but she asked if we wanted to join them."

Her father nodded. "Whatever you want to do is fine with me."

"I told her yes."

Stan laughed and winked at Michele. "Then it's already decided. Maybe we can run by the hospital first. Paul Rossi's spending all his time with Alice. They're hoping she'll be released in a day or two."

"That's wonderful news." Michele checked her makeup in the hall mirror. "I baked cookies. Why don't you take some to the hospital? The Hughes children might like some, too."

"Where are you and Jamison going tonight?" her father asked, watching as she refreshed her lipstick.

"He's taking me to dinner at the club, but he's been a bit secretive." Michele knew her cheeks were flushed with excitement. She felt like a high school girl on her way to the prom.

Moving to stand next to her husband, Roberta smiled as if she, too, had a secret.

Michele glanced at her mother. "Do you know anything about what Jamison has planned?"

"Why, no, dear."

"I don't believe you, Mother." Michele laughed, feeling even giddier as the doorbell rang.

"I'll get it." Stanley opened the door and extended his hand to Jamison. "Good to see you, son. Michele said you two are going to the club tonight."

"Yes, sir." Jamison accepted the colonel's handshake and stepped inside.

Dressed in a dark suit and a red tie, he looked better than any prom date, and Michele had to remind herself to breathe. His white shirt was starched and as bright as the smile that lit up his face when he saw her standing in the hallway.

"You look beautiful," he said, sounding somewhat breathless himself.

"Thank you." She stepped into his arms and kissed his cheek. "And you look handsome in your new suit."

"What time are your reservations?" Roberta asked.

"Six-thirty, ma'am."

"We'd better be going." Michele reached for her purse. "Mother and Dad are having dinner with Curtis Hughes and his sister-in-law and children this evening."

"How are the children?"

"Adjusting. Curtis is optimistic about the future. I heard the MP who was injured has improved, as well."

"Yes, ma'am. He should make a full recovery."

"What about you, Jamison? Did you see the doctor?"

"The wound's almost healed."

Roberta smiled. "I'm so glad."

Stanley held the door open. "We don't want to hold the kids up, Roberta."

Michele laughed as she hugged her mother and dad. Accepting Jamison's outstretched hand, she walked with him to his car. The ride to the club took less than ten minutes. When they stepped into the foyer, Michele turned toward the main dining room.

Jamison caught her arm and pointed her in the opposite direction. "Our reservations are for the Lincoln Room."

"Really?" The room, decorated in dark mahogany, was a favorite of hers and usually reserved for small, private functions.

Jamison placed his hand on her back and guided her through the outer reception area. "I wanted to do something special."

Opening the door to the private room, Jamison bowed with a flourish and invited her into the dignified parlor.

In front of the mammoth fireplace, a round table, draped in a linen cloth, was set for two with fine china and silver and lit candles.

Instead of a blazing fire this summer day, the hearth contained a huge bouquet of flowers more gorgeous than Michele had ever seen. Carnations and gladiolas and lilies and baby's breath and daisies mixed with roses—red and white and coral—into an exquisite arrangement that made her want to cry as well as laugh with joy.

"Flowers are important to a woman," Jamison stated matter-of-factly. He raised his brow and kissed her lips. "Which I learned almost too late."

He wrapped his arm around her waist and ushered her toward the table, where he reached for a rectangular box and placed it in her hand.

Her heart pounded, and her mouth went dry. She couldn't talk, even if she had known what to say. So many emotions mixed through her, all good.

"Open it," he prodded, his eyes twinkling.

She lifted the top and smiled, seeing the Cross My Heart necklace.

"I found it in the training area near a yellow rose petal that led me back to you." Jamison's voice was suddenly husky, no doubt with his remembering all they had been through. "I replaced the chain with something more sturdy."

"It's beautiful, Jamison." The new chain would last a lifetime.

"Before we sit down, there's something else I want to show you."

She waited as he dug in his pocket. Her heart fluttered like a butterfly, searching for a place to land. The look on his face was full of expectation and added to the tingle of excitement that teased her neck and sent delicious waves of energy scurrying along her spine.

Time stood still as he pulled forth a small box. His strong fingers reached for the object, hidden inside, that he held up for her to see. A beautiful solitaire diamond ring. The radiant stone sparkled in the candlelight and reflected the love she saw in his eyes.

"Michele, I'm asking you to be my wife. It won't always be candlelight and roses, but if you'll have me as your husband, I promise to honor you and cherish you and love you all the days of my life."

Her eyes burned and a lump formed in her throat. "Oh, Jamison." She couldn't talk for a long moment as she looked at him, seeing the good man, the honorable man, the righteous man he had always been. She had just needed to look beyond her fear to see the possibility of a future together.

Extending her left hand, she smiled as he slipped the ring on her finger. "I would be honored to be your wife," she said, gazing into his eyes. "I promise to love you and cherish you and go wherever you go for the rest of my life."

She stepped into his arms, feeling his strength and his gentleness at the same time. They had a lot to learn about each other, but God would give them time, a lifetime together.

Jamison had taught her to live in the present and be grateful for every blessing the Lord provided. Life was a mix of joy and sorrow. Theirs would be no different, but she no longer had to fear God or the future.

"I belong in your arms," she sighed as he lowered his lips to hers. Jamison kissed her as if he never wanted to let her go, and she knew what they had together was more perfect than any diamond or flower or the fine china or anything else the world might offer in comparison. They had chosen the better portion, the love that would last a lifetime and carry them into eternity. Which is how long she wanted to stay wrapped in his arms.

"How long is eternity?" she asked.

"Not long enough." And then he kissed her again and again and again.

* * * * *

Dear Reader,

The Colonel's Daughter is the third book in my Military Investigations series, which features heroes and heroines in the army's Criminal Investigation Division. Each story stands alone so don't worry if you haven't read the first two books. But if you enjoy this story, be sure to read *The Officer's Secret,* book 1, and *The Captain's Mission,* book 2.

In *The Colonel's Daughter,* an army wife has been murdered at Fort Rickman, Georgia, and Special Agent Jamison Steele needs to solve the crime, which puts him face-to-face with Michele Logan, the woman he once loved. Michele left him ten months ago without even saying goodbye, and now she's back on post and in danger.

Michele and Jamison struggle with mistakes they have both made in the past that must be revealed and healed before they can have a chance at love. Jamison puts his trust in the Lord and relies on a firm foundation of faith to get him through the darkest times. Michele, on the other hand, feels abandoned by the Lord and struggles to make sense of the pain in her past. I hope the Lord is your firm foundation in times of trouble. Our God is a merciful and loving Father who wants the best for His children. Turn to Him in your need, and you will never be disappointed.

I'd love to hear from you. Email me at debby@debbygiusti.com or write me c/o Love Inspired, 233 Broadway, Suite 1001, New York, NY 10279. Visit my website at www.DebbyGiusti.com and blog with me at:

www.seekerville.blogspot.com
www.craftieladiesofromance.blogspot.com
www.crossmyheartprayerteam.blogspot.com

Remember, I'm praying for you!

Wishing you abundant blessings,

Debby Giust

Questions for Discussion

1. Jamison talks about the mistakes he has made in his life. Which mistake troubles him the most? Why?

2. What was the underlying problem between Michele and her mother? Why did they hold on to their pain for so long?

3. How did each person in Michele's family react to Lance's death, and what did Michele learn in the end?

4. Why was the military important to Jamison?

5. In hindsight, do you think Michele made the right decision to help with the coastal relief effort or should she have visited her brother?

6. Have you been to a welcome-home ceremony for returning military? What emotions did you feel seeing the joyful reunions, whether you watched in person or on television? Did this story capture some of the emotions you experienced?

7. Why did Michele struggle in her faith? Have you ever had a time when your faith faltered? What or who helped you return to the Lord?

8. Michele keeps a small plaque in her dresser drawer that contains a quote from scripture: "All things work together for good to those who love God." Romans 8:28. How does that verse apply to this story? Have you found it applies to your life, as well?

9. Who were the positive role models in Michele's life? Who were Jamison's role models? Who has made a difference in your life? Have you been a role model for others?

10. Why did Michele feel responsible for her brother's death? What did she need to realize?

11. When did Jamison develop such a strong foundation of faith? How did that help him cope with difficulty?

12. Why did the E.R. clerk call Jamison a superhero? What did that reveal about her own life? How did her comment affect Michele?

13. Military wives are supportive of one another, especially when their husbands are deployed. How was that brought out in this book? Do you have military families in your area that may need help? How can you reach out to them?

14. What is the turning point in Michele and Jamison's relationship? When did Michele realize she loved Jamison?

15. What did you learn from this story?

REQUEST YOUR FREE BOOKS!

2 FREE RIVETING INSPIRATIONAL NOVELS
PLUS 2 FREE MYSTERY GIFTS

YES! Please send me 2 FREE Love Inspired® Suspense novels and my 2 FREE mystery gifts (gifts are worth about $10). After receiving them, if I don't wish to receive any more books, I can return the shipping statement marked "cancel". If I don't cancel, I will receive 4 brand-new novels every month and be billed just $4.49 per book in the U.S. or $4.99 per book in Canada. That's a saving of at least 22% off the cover price. It's quite a bargain! Shipping and handling is just 50¢ per book in the U.S. and 75¢ per book in Canada.* I understand that accepting the 2 free books and gifts places me under no obligation to buy anything. I can always return a shipment and cancel at any time. Even if I never buy another book, the two free books and gifts are mine to keep forever.

123/323 IDN FEHR

Name	(PLEASE PRINT)	
Address		Apt. #
City	State/Prov.	Zip/Postal Code

Signature (if under 18, a parent or guardian must sign)

Mail to the **Reader Service:**
IN U.S.A.: P.O. Box 1867, Buffalo, NY 14240-1867
IN CANADA: P.O. Box 609, Fort Erie, Ontario L2A 5X3
Not valid for current subscribers to Love Inspired Suspense books.

**Are you a subscriber to Love Inspired Suspense
and want to receive the larger-print edition?
Call 1-800-873-8635 or visit www.ReaderService.com.**

* Terms and prices subject to change without notice. Prices do not include applicable taxes. Sales tax applicable in N.Y. Canadian residents will be charged applicable taxes. Offer not valid in Quebec. This offer is limited to one order per household. All orders subject to credit approval. Credit or debit balances in a customer's account(s) may be offset by any other outstanding balance owed by or to the customer. Please allow 4 to 6 weeks for delivery. Offer available while quantities last.

Your Privacy—The Reader Service is committed to protecting your privacy. Our Privacy Policy is available online at www.ReaderService.com or upon request from the Reader Service.

We make a portion of our mailing list available to reputable third parties that offer products we believe may interest you. If you prefer that we not exchange your name with third parties, or if you wish to clarify or modify your communication preferences, please visit us at www.ReaderService.com/consumerschoice or write to us at Reader Service Preference Service, P.O. Box 9062, Buffalo, NY 14269. Include your complete name and address.

LISUS11B

celebrating 15 YEARS

Love Inspired
SUSPENSE
RIVETING INSPIRATIONAL ROMANCE

A troubled past that can't be forgotten!

THE DEFENDERS

Someone is systematically taking everything from widow Lindy Southerland's life. First her house, then her bank account. She's scared her young son may be next. Former marine Thad Pearson knows Lindy is hiding something, and he is the only one who can protect her and her son as if they're his own family. But keeping his scarred heart safe proves his toughest assignment yet.

STANDING GUARD

by VALERIE HANSEN

Available September wherever books are sold.

www.LoveInspiredBooks.com

LIS44505